Ransom Gold

BY

MAC (O. H.) MCCLELLAND

TABLE OF CONTENTS

To easily order soft cover books and eBooks listed below, please visit www.macs-books.com. Regarding his upcoming books please contact Mac McClelland via email macmcclelland@hotmail.com

Other books by the author:

Eagle that Walks
Wind at His Back
Guilt Exterminators
Adventures of Billie Otter
Shell Shock
Critters on Holiday
A Twisted Trail
Wild Horse Hunters
Mac Flying Higher

ACKNOWLEDGMENTS

I wish to thank an old friend from high school days, Irene Follis, for the efforts she spent on editing my writing, Also for the tremendous work that my wife, Marlene did in designing the front and back cover and the even more daunting task of formatting the pages to suit the publisher's demands. Thanks, honey, we make a great team!

In all my writings, I receive a lot of support and encouragement from several of my close friends, Jim, Joe, Jan and others. Thanks a heap. Mac

ABOUT THE AUTHOR

Few people have been privileged to excel in such a diversity of career experiences as Author Mac McClelland! From his humble beginnings as a Kansas farmer, he was called into the Marine Corps during the Korean War, where he proudly served, flying jets and helicopters.

Years later as a civilian, he added yet another career in real estate sales combined with property management. Eager to work with his hands again, he jumped at the opportunity to develop skills in building and construction and for the next 41 years built and sold over 63 homes. During this time he taught his two kids, Sheila and Scott, this trade from the ground up. In fact Sheila and he built together approximately 25 homes together to resell or keep as rentals.

When Mac reluctantly began winding down from the strenuous demands in construction, his daughter Sheila encouraged him to consider writing as a hobby. Each career had contributed in some way to his education. With his ready wit he began breathing life into his words on those pages and many readers, young and old are now enlightened, entertained, and inspired with each new book.

THE CRISIS

"Attention governments and people of Los Angeles, Orange and San Diego Counties. This is no joke. All the public systems furnishing fresh water to this area, have been poisoned! The water is perfectly safe at this point, but the poison will be released at my discretion, if the ransom money is not paid according to my instructions."

"A small recreational lake, Lake Dixon, near Escondido, California has had the poison released. By tomorrow morning, the surface of the lake will be covered with dead fish and any other creature which has partaken of the water. If anyone is using the water from this lake, I suggest you cease immediately! This is a sample of the future of Southern California fresh water supply, should you fail to comply with my demands."

"This is Irwin Clayman with LAXTV. Last evening our broadcast was interrupted by a clandestine voice threatening Southern California with destroying our fresh water supply. We were told that a small recreational lake was poisoned to show that he meant serious business. Carl Lund is on the site to give you this report. Carl?"

"I am standing on a small knoll overlooking Dixon Lake. It lies in what used to be a pristine valley on the outskirts of Escondido, California. Folks, I can't begin to describe the horror that has overtaken this area. Behind me you can see that the surface of this lake is awash with dead fish. Some of them are huge, folks. I see a lake bass fully as long as my arm, floating dead on the water. The birds which are feeding on these dead fish, have also fallen victim to this monster who has poisoned the---."

"Too bad that I must interrupt Mister Lund's tirade. This is the "monster" whom he was about to describe. It was necessary for me to exhibit my capabilities. If, Mister Mayors, you do not want the rest of your water supplies to look like this, you will immediately collect four thousand pounds in gold bars to be used as ransom. The bars will not exceed ten ounces each. You will announce on this channel at this time, when you have the gold, then I will inform you on how to deliver it to me. Please do not dawdle. The poison will be released automatically in ten days. You will need a few days to recover the canisters. To attempt to recover them prematurely would be disastrous."

Gilbert Townsend heaved a great sigh as he cut the power to the powerful transmitter that he had used to hack into LAXTV of Los Angeles. After months of preparation, his dream of great riches was about to bear fruit. Eighty million dollars!

His thoughts drifted back to that fateful night when he presented his plan to his accomplices.

The small motel room on the outskirts of Kansas City was filled with smoke. It was a warm night and the air-conditioner was unable to keep up with the burning cigarettes. Gilbert Townsend rose from his seat on the bed and crossed the room to throw open the door.

"I'm going to stomp on the next man to light a damned cigarette. I have a great plan to harvest a lot of money and I don't want to die of emphysema before I can pull it off."

The room was silent as the two men who had practically chain-smoked since arriving, guiltily stubbed out their smokes. Gilbert waited a few minutes to allow the air to clear, then shut the door and returned to his seat on the bed. His wife sat in one of the two easy chairs, the four other men sat on the remaining chairs and the second bed.

Gilbert Townsend, forty-two years old, was an adherent of physical fitness and it showed in his stocky, heavily muscled body. His shock of dark, unruly hair had just a few gray tuffs showing above his ears. At five foot ten inches tall, he was an imposing figure. His open, almost handsome features belied his life of crime. That he had never been caught or even accused of a crime was due to a higher than average IQ and an over-abundance of good luck.

Marge his wife of twenty-two years, had been a knockout in her younger days. After her only child was born, she'd gained weight and now looked older than her husband. She loved her husband deeply and would do almost anything that he asked without complaint. A placid, natural blond-haired person, she could, on occasion, play the part of the 'dumb blonde, but could hold her own in the intelligence arena. She had been able to hold herself aloof from most of her husband's illegal activities. On this caper, however, she would be a full partner.

The four remaining men were in their late twenties. Besides their age, they had other traits in common. All had served in the armed forces and had received dishonorable discharges for some type of thievery. They were proficient with firearms and had all done some boating during their short careers. They had been carefully selected by Gilbert Townsend.

"I told you earlier that you would make a lot of money if you joined me and the venture is successful," Gilbert began impressively. "I will tell you now that I am talking about seven million dollars apiece."

Gilbert waited until the furor from his announcement had subsided.

"I will be collecting the lion's share because, first it is my idea. Second, I am spending several hundred thousand of my own money up front. Has anyone any objection to that?"

"How much are we talking about, total," asked Rocco, one of the four.

"I am going to hold Southern California hostage for eighty million dollars." Gilbert stated the amount very matter-of-factly.

Complete silence greeted his statement!

"Did you say eighty million!" Wilson, a second man, asked finally.

"That's right, but it is not going to be an overnight thing. This will take a minimum of one year, probably twice that long. There is a lot of work to be done in preparation and a lot more after we get the money," Gilbert responded.

Again, he paused as several questions came at him at the same time.

"Just be patient and I will have answered all your questions before we leave here tonight," Gilbert proceeded to speak for a full hour.

"Here is a map to the place in Colorado that I have rented. I want you all there by a week from tomorrow. Bring clothes for both summer and winter. I will furnish food and lodging, anything else you will buy with your own money." Gilbert's voice was slightly hoarse from talking. "Any more questions?

If anyone has any qualms regarding this operation, now is the time to voice them. Once we are underway it will be unacceptable for any change of mind!"

A few minutes later Gilbert and Marge drove away. It had begun.

THE PLAN

It was a lovely setting, a large four-bedroom house sitting back into a glen of tall evergreen and aspen. A small stream ran by the house and into a four or five acre lake. Lake bass could be seen leaping from the water in pursuit of fluttering moths during the twilight hours. The beauty of the area belied the clandestine activities taking place there, hidden from view from any casual traveler. A locked gate at the entrance precluded any accidental visitor.

Several vehicles were parked around the front entrance, including two enclosed vans. Gilbert Townsend had his crew around him in the living room and was giving them instructions.

"Rocco, you and Wilson go into Colorado Springs and purchase one hundred, more or less, electric driven, remote controlled toy motor boats about this size." Gilbert showed them a small toy motor boat. "Try Wal-Mart, Sears, K-Mart and Hobbycrafts Inc. Only buy two or three at a time. Pick up a bunch of batteries. If you have to, drive on into Denver."

He handed each of them a handful of gift cards. "Use these to pay for them, there are two hundred fifty dollars on each of them. That should be sufficient. Take the two vans and buy gasoline with your own funds. I will reimburse you, if you save the receipts."

Gilbert then turned to Martinez and Rusty, the other two young men. "You men have a harder job."

He held up a tiny canister with a small balloon attached to it. He touched a button on a remote control being held in his other hand there was a small hiss as the balloon expanded.

"I have fourteen of these and I need eighty more. I purchased them at Unique Hobby Supplies. There is only one in Colorado Springs and two in Denver. Neither carried very many of them. Indicate that you have a secret government project that requires continued use of them and have them order more if you need to." Gilbert passed each of them several gift cards.

"Boss, when are you going to tell us how you are going to make us all millionaires," Rusty inquired.

"I have a couple of loose ends, Rusty, and then I will lay out the whole project for you," Gilbert replied. "Marge and I are taking off on one of those loose ends today. If you all get back before I do, break out some of the boats, especially of different models and try them out in the lake. It is five hundred, thirty-two yards at the longest point. I need to know exactly how long it takes each model to traverse the lake. Any questions about what you are to accomplish? I have my cell phone, but only call in an emergency."

The ancient warehouse was located in old Long Beach, California, only a short block to the water. The whole area showed its age, much as the old man who met them. Favoring a cane, he had a rolling gait as he advanced to greet them.

"Reckon you saw my ad," he remarked with a Scottish burr and held out a gnarled old hand. His other hand swept toward the back of the building where there were a number of dusty hulks, relics of another era, from a war almost forgotten. The nearest one had painted on its side in barely readable block letters, PT 547.

"I joined the Navy at seventeen in the middle of the big war and crewed one of these torpedo boats in the Pacific. I just loved them. I got my dad all enthused after the war ended. He bought seven of them as war surplus. Paid two thousand dollars apiece for them. That was a lot of money in those days," the old man continued. "He was going to rebuild them to carry people and run a high speed passenger service between San Francisco and Los Angeles. I think it would have been a success then, but he never found the money to go any further. Of course we know now, after a few years, air planes would have put him out of business, so maybe it was just as well."

Gilbert and Marge Townsend strolled among the old relics. Gilbert ran a loving hand along the curved bow of some of them as he made up his mind. Finally, he turned to the old man.

"How are the engines?"

"I light them off for five minutes every six months," the old man stated proudly. "Drain the oil every once in a while. I think they are in as good shape as when Dad bought them."

"Tell you what," Gilbert had decided. "I'll give you twenty-five thousand dollars for two of your pick, delivered at the Oceanside Marina. I have two conditions. I want a six by six foot opening in the bottom of the hull behind the cabin and the wood replaced by a heavy, clear Plexiglas. I want the Plexiglas dogged down with clamps, so it is removable. I am going to conduct tours of the reefs, besides offering high speed rides in an old PT boat."

"Uh huh. And what is the other condition?"

"Only that they be seaworthy, don't leak, etc.," Gilbert replied.

"Add two more thousand and it's a deal," the old man said shrewdly.

"I'll give you ten thousand now and the rest on delivery," Gilbert accepted.

"You bought yourself a couple of PT boats. Come back to my office and I'll give you a receipt."

"Great," Gilbert responded. "If possible, I would like to keep them under wraps until I am ready to open for business, could you deliver after dark? I could be waiting with a couple of large tarps. Those two old warriors would attract a lot of attention!"

"I understand. I will meet you in Oceanside Harbor at nine p.m. on the fifth of next month.

Gilbert smiled his satisfaction at his wife and squeezed her hand as they left the old warehouse.

PRACTICE RUN

Gilbert and Marge landed at the Colorado Springs Airport where they had left their car, and drove into the city for a brief stop at a hobby shop. Gilbert went in, leaving Marge in the car.

"Hi, I'm Roy Johnson," he told the clerk behind the counter. "You should have received my shipment by now."

The clerk disappeared into the back room and reappeared shortly, carrying a large container. He made three more trips.

"Here it is, Sir, one hundred thirty-two pounds of Aqua-Soft Resin." He set it on the counter. "That would be three hundred seventy-eight dollars and ninety-five cents with tax."

Gilbert paid him in cash and carried the containers to his car. As he picked up the last container to leave, the clerk called after him.

"Remember, Mister Johnson, don't use this on boats, as it is water soluble," the clerk called after him.

"Thank you, I'll remember." Gilbert smiled as he closed the door.

None of the others had returned when Gilbert and Marge arrived back at the cabin.

"Unpack for me, Darling. I want to run one more test before we do a mass assembly."

Gilbert raised the garage door while his wife took the suitcases inside the house. He moved over to a worktable and removed two small glass vials and a container of white salt. He then filled the vials with the salt, leaving exactly seven centimeter of space at the top. Now, he opened the container of Aqua-Soft Resin, using one of the squeeze bottles from the container, he filled the open space in the vials.

Then he placed the salt filled vials with their resin cap in a small toaster oven and turned the heat to three hundred twenty-five degrees for fifteen minutes. While the oven was running, Gilbert rummaged around for a small bucket, which he filled with sand attaching a nylon cord to the handle.

After checking that the resin was hard, Gilbert attached one of the vials to the bucket handle with a plastic tie and walked down to the lake pier. He lowered the bucket down in the water. It sank about ten feet to the bottom, then he tied the cord to a ring on a pier post and returned to the house.

Wilson was the first to show up the following day. His van was crammed with boxes of small motorboats.

"I only got thirty-two boats, Boss. It will take about two weeks for them to get more in. I think Rocco has about the same amount."

"That's fine Wilson, just start assembling them," Gilbert reassured him. "We got time."

While Wilson was unloading the model boats, Gilbert set to work with a multi-button remote control. Satisfied that he had them all set correctly, he removed a model boat from one of the cabinets. First, he taped a small explosive igniter to the hull. Next, he attached a miniature CO_2 canister, which connected to a rubber balloon and the underside of the boat. Then he placed a chunk of lead weight on top of the igniter. Last, Gilbert affixed the remaining salt filled vial to the top of the boat, well away from the igniter and canister. He used plastic tie wires to insure the vial was firmly attached.

Wilson had stopped unloading to watch at this point, as Gilbert motioned for him to pick up the remote control and follow him down to the lake.

"If all goes as planned," Gilbert explained, "I will drive the boat over to the far side of the lake and back, then sink it by blowing a hole in the hull. The CO_2 canister should bring it back to the surface when I push this button." Gilbert indicated the red button on the remote control panel.

"What if it doesn't work as planned," Wilson inquired anxiously.

Gilbert shot him an impatient look. "Then I fix it!"

The little boat sped away from the shore, driving almost to the far side of the lake before making a broad, sweeping turn to return. About a hundred feet away, the engine quit. There was a sound, much like a pistol shot and the boat sank beneath the surface. A few bubbles of air rose to the surface, and then, all was quiet.

Anxiously, Gilbert pressed the red button. There was a disturbance in the water where the boat had disappeared, and the boat popped to the surface. It was floating on an air-filled rubber pillow. A broad grin appeared on Gilbert's face as he waded out to retrieve his invention.

"If that resin works as advertised, we are all set," he exulted, as he set his ruined toy on the ground.

"The way it will go down, is that we launch the boats with the canister filled with poison," Gilbert continued. "This little igniter blows a hole in the hull and the lead weight sinks the boat. If the boat is undisturbed, the resin melts and releases the poison. However, assuming they pay the ransom, I will fly over and set off the CO_2 canister which inflates the cushion and floats the boats back to the surface. The Water Authority can retrieve the boats and poison.

THE LAW

Adam Waterman had a passable singing voice. Not good enough for professional singer, but good enough for the church choir, where he sang second tenor. He was participating in a beautiful contemporary piece called, "Majesty", when his cell phone vibrated.

He waited until the song was finished and the choir was seated, before peeking to see who had called. "Dang", he muttered to himself, as he rose to his feet and excused himself to his fellow singers and edged out of the choir loft. Once out of hearing of others, he stopped and dialed the offending number.

"I'm sorry, Detective, I know you are at church, but the captain says to get here ASAP." Adam recognized the voice of Sergeant Rogers.

"What's going down, Rogers?"

"I don't have time to explain, if you please, Detective. I got a lot of calls to make," Sergeant Rogers explained and hung up.

Adam Waterman, at twenty-seven years old, had advanced rapidly in the Los Angeles County Police Department. Five foot eleven inches, his lanky form seemed larger in his dark suit, the required uniform for detectives in the Department. His jaw was too prominent, and his nose was a little too large, which prevented him from being handsome. His only draw for the opposite sex was his look of extreme masculinity. His face and arms were deeply tanned, due to his hobby of roaming the hills in search of semi-precious stones.

Born in Valley Center, California, a small community on the edge of the foothills of southern California, he loved roaming around the hills as a young lad. He had a large collection of stones, gathered during his wanderings. He attended Vanguard Christian College graduating at the top of his class. He then took a yearlong course in Law Enforcement, his first love, before applying for a job with the Los Angeles County Police Department. He scored high on the test scores and was hired.

As a rookie, he faced an armed robber, who used a woman hostage as a shield. Adam fired one shot through the robber's head, ending the confrontation. Later, at the hearing, he was criticized by a commissioner for risking the life of the hostage by shooting over her head.

"My shooting was of no danger to the hostage," Adam maintained.

"How can you say that," the commissioner demanded. "You were fifty feet away!"

"Because I can put seven bullets in a target the size of your hand at fifty feet," Adam replied coolly.

The hearing recessed and the Board of Inquiry moved to the shooting range, as the commissioner accepted Adam's challenge.

Not once, but twice, Adam shot the center out of the target, easily covered by a man's hand.

The commissioner threw up his hands in surrender, and hereafter became an ardent supporter of Rookie Waterman. His support, plus Adam's high-test scores, contributed to Adam's rapid advancement.

Fully a dozen officers had crowded into the Captain's office, when Captain Walker strode in. He held up his hand for quiet and waited until the voices quieted.

"Be quiet now, and listen to this tape."

"Attention governments and people of Los Angeles, Orange and San Diego Counties. This is no joke---"

Captain Walker let the tape play out and shut it off.

"As you have just heard, there is hell to pay! How we are going to react to this is way above my pay grade, but if any of you or your contacts has heard a sniff of anything connected to this madman, I need to know about it. We haven't much time. Get me some answers! Be back at eight o'clock tomorrow morning."

Several voices began to speak at once.

"Captain, what if—"

"I don't know a thing more than you just heard. We just need to follow normal procedures at this point," the captain interrupted. "It is rumored that the governor may reply on television tonight at six o'clock." "Detective Waterman, I need to see you in my office, now," Captain Walker added, as he headed for the door.

"Shut the door and grab a seat, Adam," Captain Walker called from behind his desk as Adam knocked at his door.

Captain Walker began to speak without preliminaries. "They are forming up an inter-service task force to run this madman to ground. I volunteered you from this department."

"Gee, I don't know, Captain. Will they give in to his demands?"

"We don't know yet what his demands are going to be. He is serious, and he did poison Dixon Lake. It is a terrible mess. Whatever he asks for, he will get. We will pay," the captain declared. "He is expected to tell us what he wants tonight."

"I really don't think I'm fitted for this, Captain. This is way out of my league."

"Adam, this is way out of all of our leagues. I need you to represent this department with the FBI, or whoever will be in charge. You are a perfect fit. You're intelligent, resourceful and you can think out of the box. That is what is going to be needed on this case." The captain paused for breath. "This isn't going to be over when we meet his demands! Not by a long shot! We will find this SOB who dares to threaten us. You take this job and help run him down!"

Adam gave in "I'll do the best I can, Captain."

Adam Waterman was in the captain's office along with several of his staff with the television turned "on" and tuned in to LAXTV, listening to the six o'clock news.

"**..... Mister Mayors, if you do not want the rest of your water supplies to look like this, you will immediately collect four thousand pounds in gold bars to be used as ransom. ....**"

The listeners stared at each other in shock! "Four thousand pounds in gold bars," someone repeated incredulously, as the broadcast finished.

Irwin Clayman immediately introduced the Governor of California, who obviously had been standing by with a prepared speech.

"I am directing these remarks to the monster, who is threatening our water supply. We will make every effort to meet your demands. I have set up a special hotline, direct to my office. Eight hundred five five five dash six zero zero zero. I hope you will contact me personally, so that we can make the necessary arrangements."

Mister Clayman then reappeared on the screen to rehash what had just been heard. Captain Walker reached over and shut off the television.

"Where can they get four thousand pounds in gold bars within ten days?" Sergeant Rogers was the first to speak.

"Fort Knox! That would be the only place. It will take presidential approval," the captain replied without hesitation.

13

"How on earth can they spend that many gold bars without getting caught," Adam wondered.

"Those are the key words." Captain Walker grimaced. "Without getting caught!"

"Let's call it a night." The captain slid his chair back. "Adam, you will probably get a call from somebody tomorrow. I gave them your name and phone number."

Adam nodded as they filed out of the office.

Adam was shaving the next morning when his cell phone jingled.

"Good morning. This is Dick Nesbitt with the Federal Bureau of Investigations in Washington. I apologize for the early call, although it is ten o'clock here."

Adam assured him that he was awake and bushy tailed, ready for business.

"Your name came with high recommendations," the voice continued. "I need a chore accomplished, ASAP. We need a sample of the water supply from the poisoned lake. Dixon Lake, it is called. Do you know where it is? Could you get one today and meet our courier plane in Los Angeles Airport this evening?"

"I know the lake, it is about a five or six hour round trip, depending on traffic. Hopefully, I could be at the airport by three or four this afternoon," Adam responded.

"That would be great. Just hang out in the front of the security area; my boy will look you up. He has your photograph," the voice replied. "One more thing, if you could pick up a small fish carcass, also, that would be helpful. We are trying to run down where the poison was purchased."

Adam restored the cell phone to his pocket and thoughtfully studied his image in the mirror. "You are getting into deep water here, son. Are you up to it?"

Gulping down a fried egg, sausage and English muffin sandwich washing it down with black coffee, he checked his watch.

"I'll be right in the middle of the rush hour traffic. Oh well, once I get to the freeway, it will be mostly the other way. Whatever," he muttered to himself.

14

In spite of the macabre description of the destruction at Dixon Lake, Escondido, California, by the man on television, Adam was unprepared for the sight of thousands of dead fish floating in windrows, next to the shore. City workers wearing masks, raked in the rotting carcasses and loaded them into trucks to send to the disposal areas. The stench was horrific.

Adam wasted little time in collecting his specimens, departing the scene of desolation. To a man who loved nature and the outdoors, it was a painful experience.

"Those bastards, all this for a bunch of money that they will probably never live to enjoy." He thought as he drove away.

It was almost five o'clock when Adam entered the security area. There was a long line of travelers waiting to get through the scanners. A young man in khaki coveralls approached him immediately.

"You are Adam Waterman, I believe. I am Dennis Fry, a pilot for the FBI. You have a package for me."

As they shook hands and Adam handed him the bag of samples, the young man grinned. "I work mostly for Dick Nesbitt. Probably see a lot of you in the future."

RANSOM PAID

The two garage doors were open and the five men were hard at work, assembling the toy motorboats and installing the accouterments to them. Gilbert Townsend personally installed the vials containing the poison on the boat. The resin stopper had proven satisfactory, commencing to soften at two weeks and to release the poison between eighteen and twenty days.

As the assembly was complete, the boats were carefully stacked into one of the vans with bubble wrap to prevent damage. About mid-afternoon, Gilbert stopped the work and moved over to an ice cooler. He selected a soda from the cooler and leaned against the door jam.

"Now listen up and I'll lay out the plan. As you may have ascertained by what you have been assembling, we have the capability to send these boats out into the lake or reservoir and sink them along with the poison. When I am ready, I will fly over the waters in a light plane and activate the float assembly by remote control to bring them back to the surface."

"When we are finished with the assembling, we will drive to Southern California and scatter the poison into five known water supply reservoirs. One, Dixon Lake, near Escondido, will not have stoppers in the poison vials and will kill everything in the lake.

"I will then make a couple of broadcasts on television with my threats and instructions. Their instructions will include taking the ransom gold to the west side of San Clemente Island, where we will be waiting with two old PT boats. They will transfer the gold to the PT boats, or will think they have. I have purchased them with a trapdoor in the boat's bottom. Rusty and Wilson will be driving the boats and will simply lower the gold on down through the trapdoor and onto the ocean floor. After the others have left the area, Rusty and Wilson will drop a lighted buoy over the gold, activate the GPS automatic pilot on the boats and turn them loose. The now empty boats will proceed south at high speed. Of course, everyone will assume the gold is aboard and watch them closely with radar, however, they will sail for about five hours into Mexican waters and self-destruct."

"Rocco, Martinez and I," Gilbert continued, "will be hidden in a small dark cove nearby with another boat, and after the others are safely out of sight and sound, we will move over to pick up Rusty, Wilson, and the gold and sail back to Long Beach. We will transfer the gold to two flatbed trailers and drive them to our hiding place. That's the gist of it. Any questions?

"Yeah, Boss. Where is our hiding place," Wilson inquired.

"I'm not ready to reveal that," Gilbert replied. "I don't want any hint of that to get out. Marge doesn't even know yet."

"What are we going to do with the gold, once we have it? You can't just stop into a restaurant and plunk down a ten ounce bar and ask for a T-bone steak, medium rare." Rocco looked around, grinning to see if anyone appreciated his humor.

Gilbert smiled faintly. "You are so right, Rocco, and you all will have to be patient and quiet while we reduce and convert the bars into spending money. Besides the law, we will have every gang with a couple pistols out looking for us, to share our good fortune."

Four days later, a small caravan departed the Colorado cabin. Destination, California.

It was almost midnight. A pale quarter moon shone down on the steel gray van, which was parked on the shore of Mono Lake. Mono Lake was one of the primary sources of water for the Los Angeles Basin. Several figures were unloading objects from the van, and carrying them to the water's edge.

"Be careful not to break any," Gilbert warned. "We must leave no trace on the land or in the water." One by one, he activated the remote controls and sent the little toy motorboats speeding out into the lake with their deadly cargo. Some of them must sail several miles before being sunk and dropped to the bottom of the huge lake. At last, the last boat disappeared below the surface, and Gilbert with the others, climbed back into the van and drove away.

This scene was repeated at three other locations, before the two vans and a sedan met back at the motel. The last two locations, Lake Henshaw and Dixon Lake in San Diego County, were left until the next evening. It was late afternoon of the fourth day when the jet cargo plane touched down at the Los Angeles International Airport. The plane was directed to a small hanger, isolated from the main area. The wide loading ramp dropped down from the back of the plane as it came to a stop.

Two armed Humvees with their machine guns manned, rolled down the ramp and took stations on either side of the plane. Two columns of men in camys and carrying rifles, trotted after them. They lined up between the plane and the hanger doors, facing outward. Last to disembark was a large forklift tractor. It carried a canvass-covered pallet and drove inside the hanger, disappearing shortly, before it reappeared to re board the aircraft. The Humvees followed and the ramp was closed.

The cargo plane, having kept its engines running, quickly taxied away toward the take-off runway. One of the columns of men entered the hanger; the other column surrounded the hanger. The men dropped to one knee with weapons to the ready. The entire operation lasted less than fifteen minutes. The gold was delivered and guarded.

The Governors face was noticeably haggard from stress and lack of sleep as he announced that the gold was in Los Angeles, awaiting delivery. The "monster" cut in on the broadcast before the governor finished speaking.

"You will have the ransom transported to the Long Beach Pier and put aboard a sea going scow. The scow will have a crane, capable of raising two thousand pounds. The ransom will be in two pallets, exactly five by five foot and I mean exactly! You will monitor this channel and I will give further instructions at midnight."

At midnight, LAXTV programming was again interrupted.

"The gold will arrive from the north on the west side of San Clemente island at precisely three o'clock this morning. Have all lights on the scow burning. You will be guided to the mooring site and given further instruction

All were waiting when Gilbert and Marge arrived, loaded down with pizza, salads and soft drinks. When he was relieved of the food, he slid his arm around his wife.

"How did the broadcast go," he inquired.

"Couldn't be better," Rocco exclaimed. You came in about three decibels above the newscaster, Clayman.

"You were marvelous, dear," Marge added.

"Do you think they will pay up," Wilson asked anxiously.

"No question," Gilbert exulted. "They don't dare refuse. It is just a matter of how quickly. They will have to tap Fort Knox for that amount of gold bars. Here is the disc with my last messages on it," he added, handing the disc to his wife. "You just need to play it at the appropriate times. I will have to be on that scow and hid out behind the island."

18

"Rusty, you and Martinez drive on down to Oceanside tonight. Wilson will go with you and bring the car back. Wilson, come straight to the pier. Be here before two p.m. I will sail at three o'clock. Rusty and Martinez, keep the PT boats covered over until it's time to leave, about eleven o'clock. You need to be in place before my last broadcast. Have I forgotten anything?" Gilbert's face showed the tension that he was under.

They slept until late morning and after a quick breakfast, Gilbert made ready to drive down to the pier.

"I'll take one of the vans with the trailer. Marge you bring the other one down to the pier, after the last broadcast," he instructed his wife as he was leaving.

Upon arriving at the Long Beach Pier, Gilbert found the owner of the scow that he had rented, pacing nervously on the pier next to his waiting scow. A look of relief flooded over his face as he saw Gilbert and his two men approaching.

"Good afternoon, Senor. The boat is waiting for you."

"Good afternoon, Senor Rojas. Thank you for waiting." Gilbert pulled a handful of currency from his shirt pocket. "Here is the other thousand that I promised you. We will take her out now."

Gilbert, taking the helm, eased away from the pier and headed out toward open sea, steering for San Clemente Island. It was close to sunset when he slid into the small cove, where he would wait the gold to arrive. He eased the scow toward shore until the bow rested upon the sand. They dropped anchors, fore and aft and shut down the engine to wait. It would be a long eight hours. They all stretched out on bunks to try to get some rest.

Their rest was interrupted by the muted roar of the powerful PT boat engines as they approached the transfer site. Rusty and Wilson, who were piloting the boats, cut the engines and drifted into the predesignated sites to await the expected scow. It was just before midnight.

Only the sound of the sea disturbed the night air as Gilbert and his men waited for the gold bearing scow to appear. Sleep was forgotten as the men checked their watches willing the time to pass. Would three o'clock never come?

Finally, the keen ears of Martinez picked up the sound of a throbbing engine. He waited until it was within a few hundred yards before turning on his lights and starting his engine of his PT boat. He pulled out of his mooring spot until a flashing light aboard the approaching scow alerted him that they had him in sight. He then retreated to his previous location, backing it in, and killed his engines.

Rusty, armed with a powerful flashlight and an electronic megaphone stepped on deck of his boat.

"Pull alongside and lift a pallet onto my deck. I will direct it," he called over the speaker.

Obediently, a crane appeared, carrying a covered pallet on its chain hook. It lowered the pallet with Rusty guiding it through the upper deck to the hull. Rusty dropped down and directed the pallet onto a cargo net, which covered the six by six hole in the boat's keel. As the cargo net took the weight of the gold-filled pallet, Rusty released the hook, and climbing back on deck, signaled the scow.

The procedure was repeated on Martinez's boat and Rusty called again on the megaphone.

"Continue south until clear of the island and proceed directly to Long Beach Pier."

As directed, the scow moved off and soon disappeared around the southern end of the island.

Unseen by the crew and onlookers on the scow that delivered the gold, Rusty and Martinez connected the cargo nets, which were supporting the pallet of gold to a small winch and lowered the gold through the opening in the boat's keel to the ocean floor. Rusty tossed a lighted buoy over the site, and then they started up the boat engines.

They then set the automatic pilots to twenty-eight knots of speed and one hundred and thirty three degrees in direction and dove over the side. The two boats slowly increased their speed with all their running lights lit, soon sailed out of sight.

Gilbert eased his scow carefully over the lighted buoy and dropped his own crane hook. Rusty and Martinez, who were swimming there, dove down to the pallets and soon they rode the dripping pallets to the surface and on board the scow.

It took less than a half hour before the gold was safely aboard the scow. With his running lights still doused, Gilbert slowly eased his vessel around the island and directed it toward Long Beach. One by one, he turned on his running lights. Dawn was at hand when he reached his destination. His two vans with their flatbed trailers were waiting for him. The vans, each towing a small flatbed trailer were waiting for his boat. The crane quickly deposited a pallet on each trailer. Gilbert Townsend, the skipper of the scow, stepped ashore to confront the owner of the boat.

"I paid you two thousand dollars for the use of your tub. I will pay you an additional two thousand dollars in thirty days, if you keep your mouth shut." The light from the pier glistened on a nine-millimeter machine pistol.

"If you do blab anything about tonight's doings, I will return and put a slug in your belly! Understand?"

"Yes, Senor. My mouth, it is sealed," the owner assured him.

The five men climbed into the vans and drove away.

THE GOLD DISAPPEARS

FBI agent, Dick Nesbit, with two assistants, had flown in from Washington D.C. the same day as the gold had arrived. The courier jet plane was standing by in case the trail of the gold would develop. Nesbit had sent his assistants on the scow with the gold, while he and Adam Waterman had visited the Naval Tracking station, located on a small rise near the Los Alamitos Naval Air Station. The radar operator was giving them a running commentary of what he was seeing take place.

"I have a blip moving from near the island to meet our boat. It turns back and appears to park, ah! There is a second blip next to him. The blips merge. Our boat follows and all three of the blips merge and stop. There is a lot of ground clutter on the screen."

The radar operator is silent for several minutes. Nesbit longed to light a cigarette, but the closeness of the quarters prohibited.

"The blips are separating." He flipped a switch. "It's our boat. It is moving south and turning around the island. Looks like he is headed back to Long Beach."

There was another short wait.

"The other two blips are on the move. Whoa! They are moving out! They are headed about one hundred thirty four degrees at a speed of twenty-eight knots. Straight as a string."

"What is out there ahead of them," Dick Nesbit inquired of the operator.

"Nothing, Sir." He pointed to a dimly lit map on the table next to him. "Here is San Clemente Island." He spun the protractor. "This is their track. If they maintain this bearing, they will eventually strike the southern tip of South America."

"They will probably turn and head in toward some Mexican port." Adam interjected.

Well, there goes the gold, and we don't dare launch an aircraft to follow them, lest they activate the poison in our lakes." Nesbit swore quietly.

"Sir, you both might as well grab some shut eye on the bunks over there," the radar operator remarked. "I get relieved in two hours. I, or my relief, will wake you if there is anything happening. I will have to switch to satellite imagery before long, as they will be out of range of my surface radar."

"I guess we might as well, Adam." Nesbit headed for the bunk. "I have been up for thirty some hours."

It was five hours later when a radar operator shook the two agents awake.

"Sir, the two blips just disappeared."

"What do you mean," inquired a sleepy Nesbit, "they just disappeared? You lost contact?"

"Yes, Sir. One of them just winked out and then about a minute later the other one disappeared."

Nesbit was wide awake now. "Was there anything else around? Were they close to shore?"

"No, Sir. About thirty minutes ago they passed three quarters of a mile east of another blip, but neither them, nor the other blip slowed down. And then the blips just disappeared. I checked our instruments. Everything is working perfectly. They disappeared ninety-seven nautical miles due west of Eugenia Point. I can get you the coordinates."

"Please, do that. Do you have any coffee?"

"Yes, Sir, and it is fresh." He pointed to where Adam had already poured two cups full.

Adam handed one of the cups to Nesbit, who received it gratefully and took a long sip.

It was early sunup, a Mexican fisherman and his sons were sailing out on an early morning fishing expedition. They heard the roar of powerful engines drowning out the sound of their own small inboard. Two large boats hove into view from the north and passed several hundred yards to the west of them. It was too far for them to make out who was driving the boats.

The big boats sped on by and disappeared into the haze. The fishermen shrugged their shoulders and continued on their way. Unseen and unheard by them, the leading boat suddenly exploded, followed a few minutes later by another explosion aboard the second boat. The two boats lost headway immediately and sank beneath the surface, commencing the long drop to the ocean floor below. A few floating wooden objects were all that was left.

EMILY

Emily Townsend was burnt out. At her father's urging, she had attended college in Boulder, Colorado, year around for two years. She was three fourths through the required courses, but the last couple of months had been a real struggle and her falling grades reflected her attitude.

"It is not by accident that there is a summer break," her counselor scolded. "Your brain cells need a rest from constant cramming. Come back after the end of the year. You will benefit from a respite in the long run."

It would never have occurred to her that her father had deliberately kept her away so that she wouldn't discover his questionable ways of earning a living.

She had grown up on the outskirts of Canon City, Colorado, on a small fifteen-acre farm. She loved the outdoors and acquired chickens, sheep, ducks and other farm denizens to care for. On her twelfth birthday, her parents presented her with a lovely spotted pony. From that time on, her waking hours were spent on the back of Freckles, as she called him. The neighbors became accustomed to seeing them fly down the back roads with her blond hair blowing in the wind.

In her junior year in high school her life was torn apart with the loss of Freckles. He sickened and died suddenly; her father thought he had been poisoned. Emily was devastated and inconsolable and the promise to buy another pony was repugnant to her. She threw herself into high school sports, winning the title of captain of her basketball team in her senior year.

Emily attained only medium height, but her piquant face and ready smile won friends easily. Her boyish figure was always an irritation to her, but didn't deter the myriad of male admirers. She had several applicants to escort her to the senior prom.

Going twelve months a year to school curtailed her outdoor activities, much to her chagrin and served to darken her blond hair somewhat.

Aspiring to be a chemist, she was required to take several difficult courses, of which she was the only girl in the class. This only inspired her to excel, maintaining the top ten percent in the classes. This also perpetuated the inward look, when her grades commenced to sag.

Emily knew that she would get some resistance to dropping her classes, so chose to omit any mention of it when she exchanged emails with her parents. Consequently, she was unaware that her parents were no longer living in their old Canon City residence

The occupants of her home acknowledged that they had been renting for about six months and did not know the whereabouts of their landlord. The rent check was deposited into a local bank account and all correspondence was by e-mail. Emily thanked them and retreated to a local motel where she resorted to her cell phone.

"Mom, where are you? I am in Canon City. You never told me you were moving!"

The unexpected phone call caught her mother, Marge, by surprise.

"Why, Emily dear, we thought you were still in school. What happened?"

"I just needed a break, Mom. I will explain when I see you. Where can I find you," Emily replied.

"Well, daughter." Marge hesitated. "We are near a town called Tehachapi, California. It is in central California just east of Bakersfield. You will have to call us from there and we will meet you. We don't have a real address."

"Gee, Mom. That sounds so mysterious. What is going on?"

"Like you said, dear. We can explain when we see each other," Marge replied.

"Okay, Mom. I will leave right away. With luck, maybe I will see you the day after tomorrow. I love you. Bye, bye." Emily hung up and thoughtfully put away her cell phone.

That's strange. They rented out our home and moved to California without saying a word to me. I talked to Mom a week ago and she never said anything about moving! Those renters act as if they have been living here for months. I wonder what is happening. Dad has always been so evasive about his work. Maybe he does something secretive for the government. I'm sure he would tell me if he could. I'll just take my time and trundle on to, what was the name of that place? Tehachapi? Tune it in on my GPS and follow the bouncing ball.

Emily made several stops, while leisurely making her way across the country. It was well past noon when she pulled into a truck stop in the town of Mojave for gas and lunch. She was tired and hungry, but had decided to drive on into Tehachapi that day.

She noticed three large, rough looking men, sitting at the diner's bar with bottles of beer in front of them as she seated herself at an empty booth. An elderly couple was the only other customers in the diner.

They look like bad news. I hope they won't notice me!

It was not to be. Immediately she was seen, and they commenced to whisper and laugh, while staring in her direction. Two of them were trying to persuade the third of something.

Oh, please, God. No! They are talking one of them into coming over to my table!

Grinning and laughing, the man in the middle stood up from his bar stool and commenced to stroll in her direction. His eyes locked on hers.

Without hesitation, Emily grabbed up her purse and fled out the door.

On the outskirts of town, she saw a highway patrol car pull over a speeder, which warned her not to speed, yet she anxiously watched the rearview mirror for a vehicle that could contain the three men. She breathed a sigh of relief when Tehachapi came in sight and pulled in at the first motel/restaurant, she saw. She was gratified to see many cars in the parking lot; there would be plenty of people around her.

"Whoa! The place is jammed, every table taken. Wait. There is a Sir Galahad in shining leather jacket coming to my rescue. He has an empty seat and is waving me over. Don't guess I have any choice, if I want to eat, and I am hungry! He's attractive, but not handsome. Hope I'm doing the right thing."

THE SEARCH BEGINS

"Damn! Damn! Damn." Dick Nesbit exclaimed, as he and Adam Waterman left the radar room. "How could those two boats just disappear? "All this blah, blah, blah about being able to count your gold teeth from outer space, and we can't track two forty foot boats on the wide open ocean!"

Adam wisely remained silent.

"You drive, Adam," Dick directed. "I need to call my boss."

"I'm sorry to call so early, Mister Ralston, but I need some instant 'look see' on a site down Mexico way. Yes, the gold was delivered without a hitch. They loaded it aboard two old PT boats and they took off at top speed, heading due south. Yes, Sir. Kim saw them wench the gold aboard. The problem is, we watched them on radar for five hours and then they just disappeared off the scope. No, Sir. No island or other vessel for fifty miles. Could we send a drone down over the site to see if there is an answer? Thank you, Sir. Here are the coordinates. Let me know. Good morning, Sir."

"Adam, could you swing by our office?" Dick hung up his cell phone. "I want to see if we have had any response to our investigation on the poison."

Adam nodded and they drove another forty-five minutes in silence before Adam pulled into a small office complex on the outskirts of Los Angeles. The two men disembarked as the sky began to lighten. Dawn was at hand.

The printer was clicking when they entered the office. Dick walked over to check what was coming in.

"Nice timing," he commented, "this was what I was looking for."

"Developed by a company in Peking," he read. "Most potent poison on the market. No known neutralizer. Sold in this country by permit only, but is available in Mexico. Am trying to locate outlets."

"That figures," Adam muttered. "You can probably purchase it down there at any drug store!"

Dick had moved over to the coffee pot and was making a fresh batch. "Well, I'll let the home office work on that end. Let's do some speculating about this. I'm not sure how or where, but assuming they have the ransom money safely somewhere, how can they spend it?"

"I've been thinking about that, Dick," Adam answered. "Any way you look at it, they would have to break it down into small amounts. I don't know what the price of gold is today, but it must be between twelve hundred and fifteen hundred per ounce, and up to fifteen thousand dollars for a ten ounce bar."

"How about if you got it into Mexico or some other foreign country," Dick speculated.

"You better have a small army around you, if one of the mafia got a whiff of gold," Adam chuckled. "You could take it to the authorities in some cases," Adam went on seriously, "but they would relieve you of the lion share."

"Speaking of Mexico, we have got to have missed something," Dick announced. "There is no way that they would or could load the gold into two boats and both boats disappear on the open sea. I don't think that drone is going to find anything except water at those coordinates."

"I am thinking the same," Adam agreed. "We were both half asleep. Let's drive back and review the tape of when those PT boats disappeared."

"Let's go. I need a refill on coffee. You drive, Adam. You know the way."

As the two men retraced their way back to Los Alamitos Naval Air Station, the rush hour traffic kept the conversation to a minimum. They were nearing the front gate when Dick's cell phone chirped. It was Dick's head office.

"Dick, the mayor of Los Angeles just got a phone call. The poison in the lakes will be brought to the surface of the lakes at one o'clock this afternoon. He was warned that if a concentrated search was made for the "monster", he could easily replace the poison. We are to watch for a toy motor boat floating on an air bag. A vial of poison will be attached to each boat. Ninety four boats were dispatched with the poison."

"Whoa! Ninety-four?" Dick looked over at Adam and repeated the information. "What's the plan?"

"Each water district has been given the responsibility of removing the poison from their water supplies. They are instructed to bring everything in, intact. We have to get that stuff out of circulation. Incidentally, we have been unable to run down either the supplier or the buyer."

28

"We are headed back to the radar site, Boss. Both Adam and I feel that we may have missed something and want to revisit the radar tapes," Dick remarked. "I'll let you know after we look-see. Right." Dick hung up.

"A small explosion would not show up on the tape," the radar operator explained, "but a large explosion would show up as a very brief blossom. If the operator was tired or distracted for just a small window of time, he or she could miss it."

"Okay. Let's look at the tape and make sure," Adam directed.

"I just need to look at the log for exactly when the blip disappeared. It will only take a couple minutes," the operator replied. "Help yourselves to the coffee."

"Thank you. I'll do that." Dick moved over to the coffee pot.

"Here it is. Seven thirty-three. There are the two blips moving steadily south. Yes! You're right, Sir. Just a tiny blossom, but there's no doubt. Here, look over my shoulder." The operator tapped a key on the key pad.

"See? Here are the boats. Now," he hit the key again, "only one blip and this small blossom. The lead boat blows up!" The operator tapped the key a third time. "No blip now, just this blossom. That was the second boat going up. They are both gone."

The two officials looked at each other, puzzled.

"So what do we have," Dick asked.

"Maybe the gold was booby trapped," suggested Adam.

"Impossible! We wouldn't risk it. That guy wouldn't have stopped the poison," Dick responded.

"Maybe he doesn't know that the gold is at the bottom of the ocean yet," Adam said stubbornly. "Maybe he thinks it is safely on the way to South America or somewhere?"

Dick threw up his arms and turned to the radar operator. "Could you print out those last three frames for us?"

At the operator's nod, Adam added. "Before you leave it, would you show us a shot of the area where this began, where all three boats were anchored behind San Clemente Island?"

In a very few minutes, the two men left the radar room with four printouts from the radar film. As they were buckling up their seat belts, Dick looked over at Adam.

"You got something in mind, Adam. What is it?"

"Dick, nothing is adding up. Sure, you could hide a small bomb inside a stack of gold bars and the most sophisticated detector would not find it. However, I can't believe any of our chiefs that are running this operation would be so naive as to believe that the whole gang would be crowded around the gold when the bombs exploded, thus we would still get our water supply poisoned. Neither do I believe that the monster that masterminded this rip-off would send two boats to the bottom of the ocean with all his gold."

"So, your deduction, Mister Sherlock Holmes?" Dick chuckled at his own wit.

"Dick, the gold was never on those two PT boats."

"Adam, I know the two of my men that observed the transfer of the ransom gold are not Albert Einsteins. Still, they checked that it was gold bars under the canvass covers and that they were winched over to the two boats. It was less than ten minutes before those boats blew out of there, headed for South America. You are saying during that ten minute interval a ton of gold went somewhere else?"

"I don't know, Dick." Adam gave a sigh. "This guy is no dummy. My gut feeling is that gold is on its way to a safe hiding place, and it isn't beneath three miles of ocean water."

THE GOLD MINE

Gilbert Townsend pulled into the parking lot of a motel near Ontario, California, and climbed from the van. He strode back to the sedan which his wife, Marge had driven in behind him.

"Have the boys park the vans and trailers back out of sight of the highway and check in," he said, handing her the van keys. "The rooms are reserved and paid for. You all get some sleep. I need to take care of a chore. It will take me about four or five hours. We will leave before dark and drive at night. Be sure you use cash at the diner."

After double-checking that a special suitcase was in the sedan, Gilbert drove away. A short time later, he arrived at the Ontario Airport. He stopped at a small hanger away from the main terminal. The sign in front proclaimed that airplanes were for hire.

"I am Jesse Howard with the Los Angeles Water Authority," he announced to the young man that greeted him. "I called yesterday."

"Yes, sir, Mister Howard. Your plane is all set. I'm David Helm. I'll be your pilot. We can go now if you're ready. I need to file a flight plan."

"Of course." Gilbert handed him a map with five lakes circled in red marking pen. "I need to fly the full length of each of these water reservoirs as low as you feel comfortable. Preferably about three hundred feet. I am checking the moisture content of the air to determine the amount of evaporation that is taking place."

"I really shouldn't fly below five hundred feet," David said doubtfully. "Why are you doing that?"

"If anyone questions you about it, here is my card. Just have them call me." Gilbert handed him a business card. "We are expecting drought conditions this year. A company has developed a film that we can spray over the surface of the reservoirs which virtually stops all evaporation. Or, at least, they say it will."

"And the Water Authority is going to do that?" David looked a little incredulous.

"Well, it is a pretty pricey operation. We are not sure whether it will be cost effective," Gilbert replied convincingly. "Depending on how this test comes out, we will have to run a few more tests at different times of the day to calibrate how much water we would be saving."

"Grab your stuff, I'll meet you there." David pointed to a green and white Cessna.

They had reached the far end of the first lake. Gilbert was holding a small canvas suitcase in his lap, from which protruded a probe-like instrument. It was purportedly reading the moisture content of the air above the water. In the suitcase was a remote control that was set at the frequency of the detonators in the small motorboats. This remote was activated repeatedly by Gilbert, as they flew low over the reservoir.

Gilbert asked for a second pass across the water to double check his readings. He spotted many of his motorboats floating on the surface. Satisfied with the results, he instructed the pilot to proceed to the next lake.

Upon completing a last sweep of a small lake in north San Diego County, they returned to Ontario Airport. Gilbert paid David Helm, the pilot, and assured him of future business.

He then returned to the motel where he had left the rest of his party.

"I am dead tired," Gilbert told his wife, Marge. "Wake me after midnight. I want to get there before daylight."

It was still an hour before daylight when the caravan stopped at an all-night diner on the edge of the town of Tehachapi in central California.

"Take your time eating," Gilbert remarked over a plate of biscuits and gravy, "I need daylight to find that mine."

Wilson stopped with a chunk of ham halfway to his mouth. "Mine! What mine?"

"I bought a working mine from an old-timer. It has been producing a dab of gold, enough to keep him in grub and tobacco." Gilbert grinned wolfishly. "It is going to start producing a lot of gold, now."

Rocco, seated across from him, chuckled. "Been wondering, how we were going to turn the gold into spending money. I figured you had some scheme."

Gilbert waved away other questions. "This is no place to talk. I'll show you when we get there."

At the cash register, when they were leaving, Gilbert accosted the cashier. "I am going into the hills where my sedan can't make it. Could I leave it in your parking lot for a couple of days?"

"Sure. Lock it up, but no one will bother it," the lady assured him. "Just let me know when you pick it up, so I don't worry."

They transferred their personnel gear into one of the vans and Gilbert took the wheel with his wife in the passenger seat. She held a large map of the area.

"I have the route pretty well memorized," he explained, "but the map will keep me honest."

Gilbert drove south from the main highway, skirting the center of town. Carefully observing the speed limit, he followed a well-traveled paved street for about ten miles before turning off on a dirt road. The sun was now topping the surrounding hills, giving them a surrealistic view of the surrounding hills.

The road began to deteriorate and branch out into several questionable trails. Gilbert drove slowly, but confidently with only a couple consultations with the map. Gilbert crossed a dry wash with some difficulty, but the second van bogged down in the sand. Gilbert backed up as close as he could and produced a towrope, which they attached to the stranded vehicle. The combined efforts brought it to solid ground and the trek continued.

"I was worried about that spot," Gilbert admitted. "We are almost there. Clear sailing now."

True to his word, he soon drove into a small amphitheater. Prominent to the eye was a large pile of earth and rock next to a cave like entrance into a hill. Completely out of place with its surroundings, a fifth-wheel mobile home trailer was perched to one side of the glen. Gilbert stopped his van next to it.

"I'm sorry, Marge. It's a pigsty, but see what you can do to make it livable. You men, there are a couple of tents in the doorway. One of them will be your home for the next several months. Wilson, there is a small spring down that trail a couple of hundred yards. Grab some five gallon cans and bring us some water." Gilbert gave directions like an army general. He knew that they must be kept busy to keep from moaning about their living conditions.

Gilbert opened the back of this van and opened a large wooden box, labeled "tents". He withdrew a small camouflaged pup tent, used by the military. Beneath the tent were stacked six Smith and Wesson AR 15 assault rifles and many boxes of ammunition. He removed one rifle and a box of ammo.

"Rusty, take these up to that knoll." Gilbert pointed to a rock-covered hill nearby. "Set the pup tent up to give some protection from the elements. Keep a lookout for any strangers. I will send a relief in three hours. From now on, there will be a lookout up there during daylight hours. I want plenty of warning if someone visits us, and I don't want to be caught doing anything except normal mine excavation."

"Martinez, you and Rocco erect the larger of these tents at the entrance to the mine shaft," Gilbert continued. "Place it as close to the mine as possible."

The requirement to file a claim was to have a hole excavated ten feet deep. There was another such hole nearby. Gilbert drove one of the vans next to it. He pushed some of the brush aside and entered it. His flashlight revealed it as he had remembered. The miner had apparently discovered something to cause him to enlarge the hole to about five feet by seven feet with steps leading down. It was perfect for his purpose.

Wilson arrived with the water as Gilbert came up from the abandoned mine.

"Give the water to Marge and come help me, Wilson," Gilbert told him.

Gilbert had the tarpaulin off when Wilson returned. His whoop of joy brought the others running. For the first time, they could observe the glittering stack of gold bullion!

"This is what it is all about," Gilbert observed with a grin. "You guys hold up on erecting the tent until we get these out of sight."

Gilbert climbed down into the old mine and the others passed the gold bars down to him. He stacked the bars as neatly as he could on the uneven surface. When the flat bed was empty, Rocco drove the other van over and soon all the gold was safely out of sight.

Gilbert and Wilson were unloading one of the vans of all the personal suitcases and gear belonging to the men, when Marge approached.

"Gil, the batteries are reading low, so you need to start the generator. I need more cleaning supplies. I need to buy groceries, too, if you want me to feed this crew."

"I know, Hon. We'll drive back to town when I get this van empty. I want to trade the sedan for a four-wheel drive pick-up. We will leave in about a half an hour."

"Wilson, you and the others put your sleeping tent in front of this old mine so as to cover up the signs of traffic. That will also be your outhouse. I'll pick up some quicklime in town. You will find some MREs (Meals, Ready to Eat) in the mine. Be late afternoon before we get back," Gilbert directed. "Don't forget to relieve Rusty."

Arriving at the restaurant where they had left the sedan, Gilbert moved the trailer from the van to the sedan and sent Marge on to the store.

"I'll meet you at the edge of town at four o'clock."

Gilbert proceeded to a car dealership and located a used pickup that he liked. He made a deal, trading the sedan and trailer in, barely making it to their rendezvous by the appointed time. Marge was waiting for him and followed him back to the mine.

They were gratified to find both tents in place with all the personal gear stored. Rocco was on watch and had warned the others of their approach.

Martinez had spent some time as a cook so volunteered to help Marge finish cleaning the trailer and prepare the evening meal. This won a smile from Marge, who was showing the effects of a long day.

There was little conversation during dinner as the men were hungry and tired. Gilbert sat back and lit his pipe.

"Tomorrow we become miners. You probably saw the red machine in the mine. Here is a Stryker. It pulverizes the rocks and turns them into fine sand. The rocks must be four inches or less. That's where the sledgehammers come in. One of you use the jackhammer on the wall where the previous owner was taking out ore. One will use the sledge to reduce the rocks to size, the third will run the Stryker. I suggest you rotate jobs every hour or so."

"Wilson will take the lookout post at dawn, followed by Martinez, Rocco then Rusty. I will use that manual grinder to reduce the gold bars to small bits. That job will take some finesse and I will have to practice. I intend to add a spoonful of gold to the rocks being pulverized; sifting the large pieces out before we take the mixture to the processor. Marge, take a bag or can with you on your morning walk. I need a couple of gallons of real hard stones, like flint. Something that I can use in the tumbler."

"Let's get some sleep."

THE SEARCH CONTINUES

The rest of the FBI crew was in the office when Dick Nesbitt and Adam Waterman returned from the radar site. A message awaited Dick, informing him that the pictures that the drone sent back from the site of the disappearing boats showed only open sea.

"Why I am not surprised," he muttered as he wadded the note and tossed it in the trashcan.

Adam was at one of the desks, hunched over the radar picture of San Clemente Island.

"Dick, do you have a good map of San Clemente?"

"I think so, Adam. What are you thinking about?" Dick motioned for one of the men to look up a map.

"Just thinking, Dick, if it was possible another boat was moored there ahead of time."

"Wouldn't it show up on the radar screen," Dick wondered.

"I seem to remember the radar operator mentioning a lot of clutter, plus the island itself tends to screen that area," Adam responded. "You can see on this picture how difficult it is to pick out a boat blip which we know is there."

"Bill, get a hold of the Coast Guard. See if they can run us out to San Clemente Island, say eight o'clock tomorrow morning," was Dick's reply. "Let's wrap it up for today. I'm so tired, I can't think straight."

The Coast Guard cutter was waiting at the Long Beach Pier when Adam arrived at a quarter to eight the next morning. Five minutes later, Dick Nesbitt drove up clutching a thermos of coffee. The young Lieutenant J.G., greeted them with a snappy salute. In minutes, they were roaring across the bay. There was no activity around the southern part of the island when they arrived.

"Sir, here is where the two boats were moored," the Lieutenant spoke up, as the three of them studied the radar picture.

"The map shows a little cove just past this spot." Adam scanned the shoreline.

"Right there." The Lieutenant pointed to a small inlet as the boat idled along, barely making headway.

"Could a scow or barge escape radar detection while moored in there, Lieutenant?"

The young boat captain eyed the hill overlooking the cove before answering.

"It's possible, if it hugged the shore pretty tight. I'll ease in closer. There! Those marks on the beach. Someone grounded their vessel there."

"I see what you have been thinking, Adam." Dick was excited now. "Someone parked here while the gold transfer was going on and while everyone was watching those two PT boats speed over the horizon, they picked up the gold and sailed away another direction."

"This area has continuous radar coverage," the young Lieutenant reminded them.

Dick Nesbitt threw up his hands.

"Looks like another trip to Los Alamitos," Adam remarked.

Both men were peering closely over the shoulder of the radar operator as he scrolled the tape back to three o'clock in the morning, when the gold was delivered.

"There is just too much clutter in close to shore to see anything," the operator apologized.

"Just keep zeroed in on that spot," Adam directed. "If he is parked there, maybe we will pick him up, when he moves."

They watched as the tape moved forward. The operator was the first to detect a blip emerging from the little cove.

"There she is," he remarked.

All were quiet as the blip crept over to the site of the gold transfer. It remained motionless for several minutes before following the track back to Long Beach Pier. The radar operator looked at them expectantly.

"I'll be damned," Dick exploded. "Of all the gall! They unloaded that gold onto the pier, right under our noses. All the time we were watching those PT boats sail off into the sunset. Wonder how many flat bottom boats there are on the west coast of California?"

"Oh, I don't suppose there are more than two or three thousand," Adam snorted.

Adam, along with Dick and his three assistants, spread out along the Long Beach Pier, searching for someone who was out and about at four to five o'clock in the morning. Four hours later they met at a wharf side cafe to compare notes.

"I didn't even find anyone who was up at that hour, say nothing of seeing a flat-bottomed boat sail in," was the general consensus.

"We are asking during the wrong time of day," Adam declared. "I am coming back here at three o'clock in the morning and ask the same questions."

"We will join you, Adam, but unless I have some indication that the gold was taken out of California, I have been instructed to return to Washington." Dick shrugged his shoulders. "It was assumed the gold would go to Mexico or some other country. In that case, the FBI would be needed. I think we have proven that it is still in this country, probably California."

That early in the morning, the number of individuals on the piers was much less. By five o'clock, the men were back at the cafe. There was only one report that seemed favorable. Two white vans, towing flatbed trailers, were seen in the evening. The man noticed them because they were empty and had Colorado license plates. They were gone the next morning when he was back in the area.

"Dick, could you help me one more day," Adam asked. "Help me canvass every motel in a five mile radius. We will use only what the GPS comes up with, as they would probably use that to find a motel."

"Okay, Adam. We are looking for a white van with Colorado tags. It would have checked in during the last three days. We will meet in my office at five-thirty this evening." Dick acquiesced.

Adam watched with regret, as the FBI men packed up to leave. Their search had only negative results. He felt somehow that he had failed in his mission.

Captain Walker did not give him much sympathy.

"What we do here, Detective, is to try things. When they work, we solve the problem. When they don't, we try something else. I will call a meeting of the department heads and we will just ideate. Maybe someone will have an idea or will say something to trigger an idea. Take the day off and meet me tomorrow in my conference room at nine o'clock."

At nine o'clock sharp, Captain Walker rapped on the podium.

"Get a refill on your coffee and settle down. Detective Waterman will bring you up to date on the Ransom Case. We are looking for ideas on where to go from here."

"The gold was delivered to the back side of San Clemente Island, as demanded. What seemed to happen, was the gold was transferred onto two old World War Two PT boats. Ten minutes later, the two boats took off headed south at high speed. Five hours later, they blew up and disappeared without a trace," Adam recited. "We think that, while we were watching the two boats, a third, a shallow draft craft, picked up the ransom gold and transported it back to Long Beach, where it disappeared. Our only clue, if it is a clue, is two white vans with empty flatbed trailers were on the dock that night and were gone the next morning. The vans had Colorado license plates."

"Geez. They could be half way across the country by now," someone said.

"Or in Canada or Mexico," another added.

"Why didn't they just transport the gold to Mexico on the boats," a third voice asked.

One of the detectives answered before Adam could speak. "Be real risky taking a chunk of gold like that to Mexico. If the government didn't get hold of it, the Mexican Mafia would grab it."

Adam raised his hand. "Okay, they could be anywhere now. So let's tackle it from another angle. How do they convert the gold bars into spendable cash? Any thoughts on that?"

"A lot of places buy used gold, could they somehow convert the bars to gold bracelets or something?" This was tentatively offered.

"I think you would have to combine the gold with another metal to strengthen it," was one response.

"It would take a life time to get rid of it that way," was another opinion.

"I think the most plausible way to market the gold in that quantity would be to purchase a good producing gold mine, if such a thing is available. Mix the new gold with the old, somehow." Detective Ross hadn't spoken up before.

There was silence for a minute while the others considered this.

"Doesn't Colorado have some gold mines," asked someone.

"A lot of mining going on in Idaho. I don't know about gold, though," another spoke up.

"Nevada." The detective spoke with conviction. "Lots of gold still being mined in Nevada."

"Wow! That certainly pens it down," Adam responded with a tight grin.

"I used to be in real estate," Detective Ross mentioned. "You need to check with the County Recorders or their equivalent for any change of ownership. I think most states have a department especially for mineral recovery."

"Does anyone else have any other input," Captain Walker questioned, after a lengthy lapse in suggestions.

With no response, he turned to Adam. "Adam, I will request that you be assigned as a Deputy United States Marshall to give you authority outside Los Angeles County and possibly outside the state. I feel sure they will give it to you. I can't spare anyone else from my department on a full time basis, but call if you need help for a short time."

"Men, I appreciate your input." Adam's face wore a slightly discouraged look. "Seems like I have my plate full!"

Adam spent the rest of the day on his office computer. He soon located a map of all known mining claims. He printed out the map and the list of their coordinates.

He also called the Orange County and San Diego County police departments, requesting their assistance in the hunt for the ransom gold. He got very little response except that they would check out the mining claims south of Los Angeles County, and let him know if there was any activity around any of the sites. His opinion was that the thieves would take over an abandoned mine and pretend to resurrect a vein in it.

"I won't know until I check them out," he muttered to himself.

He picked up the map and went in to see Captain Walker. "I am going to break out my Quad and check out every claim north to Tehachapi, Captain. Probably take a couple months. Maybe by that time some of the gold will start appearing on the market."

"Keep in touch. I'll let you know if anything develops here," the Captain replied.

Daylight found Adam Waterman on the road toward Borrego Springs, California, a small desert community east of Los Angeles. "San Diego said they would check everything south, so I might as well start where they quit," he told himself. Should be able to reach most of the claims with the truck until I get past Palm Springs. Then it starts to get rough, and I'll have to use the Quad. Suspect, if I can't get to the mine with the truck, however, they won't be able to carry the gold in, either."

ADAM MEETS EMILY

Tired, dirty and unshaven, Adam yearned for a hot shower, clean clothes, and a decent meal in that order. A night of rest on a mattress under a roof was next on his want list. He had been out in the hills for over two weeks and was ready for a change.

He checked into a motel on the edge of Tehachapi and took care of the first two items, but decided to just trim his beard in favor of the prospector look. He then set out to satisfy number three at the adjoining diner.

It was Saturday night and the place was jammed. A couple vacated a table set for two as Adam walked in, he claimed the table immediately. A waitress wiped off the table and dropped a napkin, silverware and water on it before disappearing.

As he waited, the door opened to admit a lovely, young, blond lady. Dressed in shorts and rumpled blouse, she showed signs of having driven a long ways.

Emily looked around anxiously for a place to sit.

Without hesitation, Adam stood up and waved to her, as if he had been waiting for her. Another quick look around without seeing any empty table, and she strode over to him.

"I've been looking for you," Adam greeted her with a sly grin, as he held back a chair for her.

"That was kind of you," she looked at him questioningly, and as Adam continued to grin, she answered him with a smile of her own. "I hope I haven't kept you waiting long."

"All of my life," Adam responded, this time sincerely, and without the grin.

"Well, the wait doesn't seem to have disturbed you greatly, but I do appreciate your inviting me to join you, since all the tables are taken."

"My pleasure, however, our waitress may have gone home, as I haven't seen her for ten minutes." Adam chuckled.

"If she doesn't come back soon, I'm going to sidle over to this gentleman at the adjoining table and ask him for a bite of his steak! I'm starved."

"I'll bet you would do it too, however you are saved from groveling to him as our waitress is coming to our rescue." Adam laughed aloud at her humor. My name is Adam, what's yours?"

"I am Emily. I am happy to meet you, Adam." Turning to the waitress, "something fast and hot. I could eat a horse, saddle and all!"

"Our lasagna is great with green salad and rolls," the waitress responded with a quick smile. "Coffee?"

"Sounds just right," Emily quickly agreed.

"Same for me. Keep it simple," Adam added.

Before they could resume conversation, the waitress returned with coffee and salad, plus another set of utensils.

Emily attacked her salad with such gusto; Adam did not have the heart to deter her with more conversation. The main course arrived before the salads were gone, so the whole meal was eaten in silence. Finally, Emily put down her fork.

"Guess I haven't been a very good dinner partner," she said ruefully.

"Well, you did mention that you were hungry," Adam defended her. "Where are you going in such a hurry that you don't have time to stop for meals?"

"It isn't that I am or was in a hurry. I stopped down at the bottom of the hill at a truck stop in Mojave. I came from Colorado and that desert doesn't have that many places to stop. Any rate, I went into this diner to order dinner. Three guys at the dining room bar turned around and just stared and stared. I tried to ignore them, but finally, I just got up and left without eating when one of them started to come over. Then they followed me out, that scared me, so I hightailed it up the hill."

"Did you notice what they were driving?" Adam looked concerned.

"No. I was too much in a--. Oh, crap! Here they are."

Three roughly dressed men walked in the door and looked around. Upon seeing Emily, one elbowed the man next to him, and they began to whisper to each other.

In one motion, Adam slid back his chair and rose to his feet. He strode over to the trio. As he neared them, he allowed his jacket to swing open, revealing the butt of his police service pistol to show in its shoulder holster.

"You are annoying the lady. Leave. Now!"

"Now wait a minute, Mister. We are just minding our own business," one of them blustered.

Adam's right hand moved to the pistol butt. "I'll not tell you again!"

"Alright! Don't get excited. We're out of here." The three men crowded out the door.

Adam followed them long enough to see them crawl into a dirty, black Ford SUV. He memorized the California license plates, a habit formed when he was a rookie cop.

Emily gazed at him wide eyed when he returned to the table. No one else seemed to have noticed anything amiss.

"What did you tell them to make them leave," she gasped.

"Aw, I just told them you were the governor's daughter, and she would tell her papa on them if they kept bothering her." Adam grinned.

"I don't believe you."

"Scout's honor." Adam held up three fingers in kind of a salute.

"That is not the Boy Scout sign and I still don't believe you." Emily didn't pursue it.

"So is this your destination, or are you going further?" Adam wanted to get the conversation back to important things.

"I am not sure. It is somewhat strange. I have been at college and I took a sabbatical to go home. I was going to surprise my folks, but the shoe was on the other foot. They were not living at home, so I called Mom on her cell phone. She said they didn't have an address, but to call them from here."

"The motel next door still has a vacancy," Adam hinted.

Emily grinned. "I think I will stay over and call Mom tomorrow morning. I'm not up to driving any further tonight."

"Then we could go out and paint the town tonight." Adam smiled back.

"Why not?" Emily laughed aloud. "Give me an hour to check in and change. My last name is Townsend."

An hour and a half later they were seated in a small cocktail lounge.

"I haven't seen much of my folks the last six years," Emily was saying, "Dad moves a lot and didn't want to make me change schools, so I stayed with an aunt near Boulder, Colorado. I am just sick of studying hard and felt I needed some time off."

"So, what does your dad do?" Adam asked, more to prolong the conversation than any real interest.

"I don't really know. Times when I asked, he just laughed and said that he was an entrepreneur and a jack-of-all-trades," Emily confessed.

"What do you do? Do you live around here?" Emily was obviously uncomfortable, discussing her dad.

"No, I live in the Los Angeles area. I am out combining a side job with a vacation. I'm a rock hound in my spare time," Adam replied.

"What on earth is a rock hound?"

"A rock hound is kind of an amateur prospector. I look for semi-precious stones, the ones that go in costume jewelry. I find them on windswept slopes and washouts. Would you like to see some of my stones," Adam asked.

"No. I don't want to go back to your room and look at 'your etchings.'" Emily laughed shortly.

Adam flushed. "I didn't mean that. I have some with me." He produced a small handful of stones from his jacket pocket.

"I am sorry." Emily reached over and touched his arm. "I took that wrong. I apologize."

"No problem." Adam spread the rocks out on the table between them. "I find lots of agate, but some are pretty dull in color. Here is a variegated one that I like." He picked one and handed it to her.

"It's lovely," Emily exclaimed. "I would just love a set of ear rings like these."

"I sell a good many of my stones to a couple jewelers I know. I could have a set made up for you. Most are done up in silver." Adam picked up another piece.

"This is another agate, called Mojave Blue. It is unique to the Mojave area. I found several a couple days ago."

Emily picked out another light blue rock. "What is this?"

"That is benitoite. It is the official California Gemstone. It is a little dull now, but sparkles nicely when cleaned up."

"Amazing! And you just pick them off the ground?"

"Well, when I find some in a washout, I will do a little digging into the bank to see what else is there," Adam replied. "That was where the Mojave Blue came from."

Adam gathered up the stones to return to his jacket pocket. In doing so his lapel swung back to reveal his pistol in his shoulder holster.

Emily gasped in surprise. "You're carrying a gun?"

"I'm sorry to shock you," Adam apologized. "I used to work for the Los Angeles police and I have a permit to carry."

"Those three goons, they saw you were armed and backed away," Emily responded.

"I'm afraid so. I didn't think I could take them on in a game of fisticuffs."

"Of course. It just took me by surprise." Emily was still a little rattled. "I think I am ready to call it a day. It's been a long one. We could meet for breakfast."

"I would like that. Call me when you are ready to eat," Adam agreed. "Here is my number. And I'll need yours to let you know when your earrings are finished."

"You aren't serious about the earrings, are you?" Emily said as she copied down Adam's phone number in her cell phone.

"Very serious. It will give me an excuse to stay in touch with you," Adam smiled.

"You are very nice. I have enjoyed our evening very much." Emily gave Adam a quick kiss on the cheek and slipped out the door.

That is one lovely lady! I can't let her slip away from me.

"Well, Adam Waterman, it was nice having breakfast with you. You are the best thing that has happened to me in a long time," Emily said frankly.

"I would so like to see more of you, Miss Emily Townsend. This has been a high point in my life." Adam wore only a faint smile.

"When I called her, Mom said thirty or forty minutes, so they must live fairly close to here. You have my phone number. I would love to hear from you," Emily responded.

"I have a few days left on my vacation. I'm keeping my motel room, we will get together again before I leave," Adam stated.

He slowly pulled her to him for a long kiss before getting into his pick-up.

She watched with regret, as he drove away.

"I do hope he calls me."

Emily walked back to the motel office and checked out, paying with a credit card.

"I am all packed, I will drop the key off on my way to my car," she told the clerk. "I may have to leave my car in your parking lot for a few days. Is that okay?"

"No problem," the clerk assured her. "You just need to park it out away from the units. We assume no responsibility for its safety, of course."

Marge Townsend had no trouble spotting her daughter, leaning against her small convertible, when she drove into the motel parking lot with her white van. Mother and daughter embraced, laughing and talking at the same time.

"Mom, what happened to your BMW?" Emily asked after the initial furor subsided.

"Oh the roads are too rough for my old car, your father traded it in on a four-wheeled drive pick-up and left me with this van," Marge replied with a nervous laugh. "We are the proud owners of a working gold mine! Throw your bags in the back. You will have to leave your little car here."

"I anticipated that. A gold mine? So are we living in a tent," Emily inquired.

"Oh no, not that primitive. We are quite comfortable in an old fifth wheeler," she nervously laughed again.

"Oh dear! I'm not sure we can accommodate that much luggage," Marge exclaimed as Emily loaded bag after bag from her car to the vehicle.

"Well, Mother, if you had let me know that you had moved from our old place, I wouldn't have packed this much."

"I know dear, it's just that--." Marge Townsend hesitated and her daughter waited for her to continue, but she said no more.

Unaware of her father's devious activities, Emily had an open mind as her mother drove. Driving on the rough road required all of Marge's attention, so the drive was mostly done in silence. Emily's first indication of anything unusual was seeing Rusty upon the knoll above the mine. He was carrying an assault rifle under his arm.

"Mom, there is an armed man up there." Emily indicated the knoll.

"I know, dear. He is one of your father's men. This is a gold mine and there is gold here. People will steal gold, you know," her mother replied. "Here we are."

GOLD BAR TO GOLD DUST

Gilbert Townsend and his crew lost no time in their efforts to reduce the gold bars into a salable commodity. Gilbert had four outlets for the gold, and they proceeded with those in mind.

He ground off minute pieces of gold bars, mixing an ounce of gold with the ore to be taken to the local assay office, who sent it on to a gold refinery. A half dozen old prospectors brought in enough to buy food and tobacco and kept the assay office in business.

A heavier amount of gold was added to the rock being ground up on the Stryker and turned into dust. The dust would be collected in heavy plastic bags. When they had a pickup load, it would be taken directly to a Tucson, Arizona, refinery.

All of the larger chunks of gold were tossed into a rock tumbler. The tumbler had been used to clean and shine semi-precious stones. In this case, Gilbert used it to knock off the rough edges and give the gold nuggets the look of gold recovered from a stream. When around fifty pounds were collected, Gilbert would transport that to Elmore County, Idaho.

The fourth outlet was in Reno, Nevada. Gilbert had purchased a defunct pit mine in a remote area not far from there. Registering the gold to that mine, he used the same system as above to produce gold granules. The only exception was to add a small amount of gravel to simulate sluice washed gold.

Wanting to establish a reason for his presence at the old mine in Tehachapi, Gilbert brought the first lot of gold ore to the local assay office.

"So old Jodie finally gave up and sold out," the old man that ran the office drawled as he accepted Gilbert's bag of ore.

"Yeah," Gilbert replied, adopting a more countrified tone, than he was used to. "I think I found a little better vein than Jodie was workin. I'm hopin you'll prove it to me."

"Wal, we'll soon find out," the old man said as he tagged Gilbert's bag and added it to a stack behind the counter. "These go out tomorrow. Have a check by Monday."

"Reckon I'll work through the weekend and see if I can have another bag by then. I gave Jodie all my cash and I'm gettin short of grub.

The old man moved over to his cash drawer and withdrew a couple of twenty-dollar bills. "I can give you a little advance. Old Jodie generally had a couple hundred in gold in each bag."

"Why, I thank ya kindly. I do miss my coffee in the mornings," Gilbert accepted the twenties and tucked them in his shirt pocket.

"Trusting old codger. Well, he will be surprised when he finds a couple of thousand bucks in that bag," Gilbert muttered to himself as he left the office. "Better fill up with gas, if I am going to Idaho tomorrow."

"That represents a year's labor for me and Ma and my three boys." Gilbert said as he set a plastic bucket on the scales. "Don't know if there's much more in that little cove."

"Feels like a mighty good years wages here, Sir. Well over a million dollars, I'd say. Price of gold is up considerably. I'll weigh it and run a purity test. Be about twenty minutes."

"I'll wait, if you don't mind."

"Of course. There is coffee and some doughnuts, if they aren't all dried out," the clerk replied.

Gilbert munched on a stale doughnut and sipped an extra strong cup of hot coffee, while he awaited the clerks return. He leafed through the Idaho Miner weekly newspaper. It mentioned several possible buyouts of small companies by a large conglomerate in Nevada.

When the clerk returned, he appeared a bit flustered.

"I must say, Sir, this is the purest gold I have ever tested. The total amount comes to One million six hundred thousand three hundred and sixty two dollars. We normally send it directly to your bank. Do you have the routing numbers and account with you?"

"Actually, I don't trust banks," Gilbert answered. "I would like five separate checks, made out to the bearer. Four checks for One hundred fifty thousand each and the balance in the fifth check."

"That is most unusual, Sir. You know, of course, that those checks will be just like cash. Very risky to carry around."

"I understand, but thanks for the warning. I am equipped to protect them," Gilbert smiled grimly.

48

"I must remember to add some fine gravel to the next batch. Guess I will have to open a bank account in Las Vegas. Taking the money in checks causes too much attention to me." Gilbert muttered to himself as he left.

Parked near his pick-up, an older Buick attracted his attention. The paint on the hood had almost a perfect circle of faded and discolored paint. The windows of the vehicle were completely tinted, making it impossible to see if it was occupied.

Gilbert didn't give it much thought, until he noticed the same vehicle three cars back behind him at the first traffic light. Even though he had ample gas for the return trip, he pulled into the first available filling station and bought ten gallons of gasoline.

He watched the Buick cruise on by, but it made a right turn at the next light. He remained at the gas pump until he saw the Buick drive by again, then he pulled out into the traffic several cars behind it. When it made a right turn at the next light again, Gilbert knew that he was being followed.

Required to wait at the traffic signal, Gilbert reached behind his seat to bring out an AK-15 assault rifle and lay it on the seat beside him. He also slid open the rear window of the cab.

"Okay, come on. Let's get it on," he said to the now invisible Buick.

As the traffic thinned out, Gilbert kept an eye in the rear view mirror for the now familiar car. He was rewarded by seeing it pass several cars and settle into a comfortable distance behind him.

With traffic almost nonexistent, Gilbert reached over and turned off his ignition switch. Holding it off for a few seconds, he switched it back on and was rewarded by a small backfire and a puff of black smoke out the pickup's exhaust. Slowing down as if he had engine trouble, Gilbert drifted to the side of the road and stopped. He left the motor running and in low gear, but set the emergency brake. The Buick slowed with him and stopped about fifty feet behind him. Gilbert turned in the seat, poking the rifle out the rear window and fired a burst of bullets into the Buick's grill. Upon striking the car's engine, the bullets turned into shrapnel, and riddled the front of the car.

Gilbert, then flipped off the emergency brake, and gunned the engine, leaving a cloud of dust and gravel behind him. The disabled Buick was soon left far behind.

Supper was over when Gilbert arrived back at the mine. The men cheered when he passed them each a check for one hundred fifty thousand dollars. It was the first money they had seen from their weeks of work. They were elated!

"Just a drop in the bucket, men. There are a couple dozen of these coming," Gilbert stated. "I have a list of banks on St. Thomas Island that are confidential. I suggest you each establish an account there. You should be able to do that on line. We can use the local library if we need a FAX. My intention is to distribute the money as it comes in, but don't get to feeling so rich that you want to quit me. I can't afford one of you running around the country with complete knowledge of our operation."

The men sobered and looked down at their feet. They took that remark as a warning, which it was!

"I need to open a bank account in Las Vegas, which I will tomorrow if the Nevada shipment is ready." Gilbert related his experience in Idaho. "I'm convinced that guy behind the counter instigated that robbery attempt."

"How are you doing on the grinding wheel?" Gilbert turned to Martinez. He had taught him how to work it on the gold bars.

"It's real tedious, Boss, but I am able to keep ahead of them. The boys let me skip a turn on the jackhammer," Martinez added.

"Your Nevada shipment is ready, boss, and the Tucson will be when you get back from Reno," Rusty chipped in. "I sure appreciate this check."

The Reno Gold Refinery accepted Gilbert's load of gold laden sand without comment. They only ask the number of the mine, where it came from. Gilbert gave them his bank account number and routing. They estimated his proceeds to be close to two million and that it would be deposited within two business days. This did not seem to be a large transaction to them.

Gilbert had made two trips to each of his outlets. There was no more trouble on the Idaho trip, and things were running smoothly until Marge received the phone call from her daughter, Emily. Marge ran to Gilbert in a panic.

"Gil! Emily just called. She is in Canon City. She is out of school for a couple of months and is coming here!"

"Damn! In addition, you told her where we were--. Of course, you did. I'm sorry, Marge. I lost it for a minute. When is she getting here," Gilbert questioned.

"She mentioned the day after tomorrow," Marge replied.

"Well, let me think. What are we doing that a regular mine would not do? We only use the tumbler occasionally. I could put it in the off shoot that caved in," Gilbert mused. "I could put up a 'Danger' sign to keep her from going in there. It is imperative that Emily not find out about the gold."

"Gil, I know you don't want her to find out that you work outside the law, but you can't hide it from her forever," Marge responded. "Your daughter is no dummy!"

Gilbert shook his head in disagreement.

"Boss, I am pretty good on that grinder, but I could work a lot faster with an electric one. I think I could produce the grains of gold in just a few hours, for a week of quartz. If you would put it in the same off shoot, I could work only when your daughter wasn't around." Martinez was standing nearby and overheard Gilbert and Marge talking.

"That would work. We'll need to cover the electric cord. Good." Gilbert gave a 'thumbs up' signal. "We have a couple of days to get it done. I'll drive in and pick up an electric grinder today."

THE ATTACK

Gilbert was waiting impatiently when Marge and Emily drove in. He strode swiftly to the passenger side and opened the door for his daughter. The smile on his face and the hug that he gave her, revealed the affection he held for her.

"Oh, Daddy, I am so glad to see you." Emily clung to him briefly as she looked around. "My! This is a surprise, but where is the gold mine?"

"The big tent covers the entrance. I will show you around when you get your gear taken care of."

"I always wanted a gold mine," Gilbert declared later. "The old prospector that sold it to me was working an old vein, but I found a better one and am doing real well."

"Tell me what you are doing here?" Emily was in the mine, looking around.

"A simple operation, really," her dad replied. "First, we jack hammer out chunks of ore and reduce it into smaller chunks to run through the Stryker. It reduces everything to sand, which we store into plastic buckets. When I have a pickup load, I take it to a refinery, they assay it and pay me money for the amount of gold in the ore."

"But I see some of the ore is in a sack," Emily remarked. "What is that for?"

"I don't want the locals to know how much gold I am taking out, so I take some of the old vein to the local assay office and he sends it off for me." Gilbert chuckled. "I take the richer stuff to Arizona where they don't know me or where the ore is coming from."

"Why all the secrecy, Dad?"

"It's a rough world out there, girl. Gold attracts robbers like honey attracts bees," Gilbert said grimly.

"You mean someone might try to rob you here?" Emily is shocked.

52

"You don't have to worry, Honey. I keep a man on guard all day long," Gilbert soothed.

Emily was tempted to tell her father about the three men who had annoyed her at the restaurant, but that would have also entailed telling him about Adam. She was not quite ready to reveal her feelings about Adam to anyone. Perhaps if, or after, he called her.

The day after Emily's arrival, Gilbert announced that he was going in to town with a couple bags of ore. He suggested Emily accompany him and check on her car.

"I'm shore glad you all are doing so good in old Jodie's mine," the old man in the assay office told them. "Sometimes his bags weren't worth sending in."

Three men were watching when Emily and her father emerged from the assay office.

"That's that uppity girl, all right," one of them said.

"Don't you worry, Otto. We'll fix her," the older one declared.

"I'll bet the guy has some money stashed away, Heinz. That's the second time we seen him at the assay office," the third one commented.

"If he does, we'll find it. It'll be just icing on the cake. Stay in here until they drive away. We'll follow them," Heinz, the older man instructed.

The men watched as Gilbert and Emily stopped at the motel and checked on Emily's car. After being assured that it was not bothering the motel establishment, but that they would assume no liability if something happened to it, Gilbert headed back to the mine. The three men in a black SUV followed at a safe distance and were unobserved.

"I know where they are headed," Heinz, the driver, suddenly exclaimed and braked the vehicle to a stop. "This is the trail to old Jodie's mine. Someone said he had sold out and left town."

"Huh! Forget about any gold. Old Jodie barely kept himself in tobacco," Otto groaned.

"Well, we'll get the girl anyhow," the driver insisted. "We'll come back with our guns tomorrow."

Emily's cell phone jingled shortly before supper that night. Her pulse quickened as the 'caller ID' identified the caller.

"Is that you, Adam," she answered the phone.

"Sure is, Emily. I will be back in town on Saturday. Could you meet me for dinner?"

"That would be great, Adam. I was hoping you would call. I left my car in town as it couldn't handle the road, but I'm sure Dad will let me use one of his vans or his pickup."

"I was wondering if you found your folks okay. Apparently you did. Could I pick you up?"

"Thanks, Adam, but it would be too difficult to try to explain how to get here. We are at an old mine that Dad acquired. There is only a trail part way."

"Okay. How about six o'clock. I will get reservations so you won't have to share a table with a stranger." Adam chuckled.

"Oh, I wouldn't mind sharing a table if I have as good luck as I did last time." Emily laughed with him.

"Thanks, Emily. Looking forward to seeing you again."

"Me, too. See you Saturday." Emily rang off.

A wave of loneliness swept over Adam as he slipped his phone back into his pocket. He was tempted to call Emily back and change the date to Friday. He had visions of them spending the Saturday wandering around town, having lunch and enjoying each other's company.

His search for the ransom gold robbers seemed fruitless. For almost a month he had been searching for some trace.

With a sigh, he reopened his map and copied the coordinates of the location of the next gold mine into his GPS. He was several miles from Tehachapi and some of the mines in the area were still working. His cover story of doing a survey for the United States Treasury Department had worked well so far, without resentment from any of the miners.

The trail he was on showed signs of recent traffic. "This must be a working mine," he mused.

Adam continued driving for another couple of miles. A dirt cloud followed him as he drove, the trail winding around to avoid the rougher ground. A vehicle appeared ahead of him. It was parked, facing back down the trail. It looked familiar as he drove on by, so he stopped and looked at the license tag. The dirt almost obscured the numbers, however the image of the three men getting into the dirty, black SUV flashed into his mind.

"This vehicle belongs to the three guys who were annoying Emily!" Adam was surprised to find the doors unlocked and he opened the glove box.

"Heinz Bauer," he read on the car registration. After a minute of hesitation, he placed a call to his headquarters in Los Angeles.

"Sally, I have a Heinz Bauer, 2006 Ford SUV Two-fifty, license LVN732J. Can you see what we have on him?"

"Sure, Detective," the feminine voice answered him. "Give me a minute." After a brief pause. "Nothing too bad. Petty theft, couple of brawls in bars. He apparently likes to fight."

"Here is a good one. A call reported physical abuse. The responding officer reported that the lady, the so-called victim, answered the door with a ball bat in her hand. She had a black eye, but her attacker was on the couch with a knot on his head the size of a golf ball." A chuckle of appreciation. "He called the paramedics. No charges were filed. Uh oh! This isn't funny. He was picked up for stalking. He got six months for that. Another charge of groping, victim wouldn't press charges. Detective, I think this is a bad one. A combination of sex abuser with an anger problem. We need to get him off the street. He is bad news!"

"Thanks Sally." Adam rang off.

After a moment's thought, Adam slid the Police Special from its shoulder holster and checked that it was fully loaded and ready to fire. He noticed three sets of tracks in the dust, heading on down the trail. He elected to follow a short distance with his truck, before driving off the road and concealing the truck in a small ravine.

"Those three goons have to be up to no good. I think I will leave my truck and follow them on foot," he mused. "Best I take my rifle and plenty of shells with me."

Adam had walked close to a quarter mile, when he heard a fusillade of shots ahead. Quickly, he dodged off the trail to gain some cover and increased his pace, but with more vigilance.

Gilbert had just finished loading his truck for a delivery to Tucson, when he heard a single shot from the knoll where Rocco was standing guard. A quick look revealed that Rocco was down and a stranger had taken his place. A shot from that stranger shattered the glass where Gilbert was looking out, stinging his face with particles.

"Get down on the floor. It's a raid," he shouted. "I have to get to the truck for my guns."

"Gil, please don't go out there," Marge cried. "You'll be killed."

"I got to. They will riddle this place. I'll wait until one of the boys open up, then I will make a run for it. If I can get to the truck, it will shield me from the rifles."

"Gil, they won't hear the shots over the noise of the and Stryker!" Marge and Emily were cowering on the kitchen floor.

She was right. They could faintly hear the jackhammer. The sounds of rifle shots were deadened by the mine enclosure.

Two rifle shots came from the pile of rocks across the clearing.

"Hey, you in the house. Send out the girl with your cache of gold and we'll let you live. You got five minutes before I turn that place into a sieve." The voice came from those rocks

"I have to go, Marge. If they get to the mine and catch our men by surprise, they are dead meat and us, too." Gilbert's face wore a look of desperation.

Another shot from the knoll made up Gilbert's mind. They would walk right in when they find out he was unarmed. He had no choice. The truck was about ten yards away. He had to try.

Gilbert swung wide the door of the mobile home and leaped in one motion. He was running hard, as bullets rained around him. One lucky bullet tagged him on the leg and he went down, rolling into the cover of the truck. The windows of the truck were the first to take fire, but he managed to get the cab door open and snatch his AK-15 from behind the seat.

Moaning in pain, he fired a short burst at the man on the knoll before turning his attention to the men behind the rocks. They had stood up to fire at him, but ducked for cover, when Gilbert's rifle slugs began to strike around them.

There was a lull in firing as the raider's assessed the new situation. One of them behind the rocks began to curse, as he realized that he had missed a chance to catch Gilbert unarmed. Gilbert listened with a tight smile. It wasn't over yet. He realized one of them would attempt to work his way around behind him.

Some way he must alert the men in the mine to theirs and his peril. The one on the knoll worried him the most, as he could move with impunity by just retreating from the hilltop. He took advantage of the lull to wrap a bandanna around his bleeding leg.

He saw some movement from the rocks, but didn't fire. The thirty-cartridge magazine in the gun that had seemed so many when he loaded it, no longer seemed so much. He must conserve ammunition.

Suddenly Gilbert heard a shot from another rifle, a louder, deeper sound. His heart sank. There is a fourth raider with a bigger rifle, not just the carbines the others were using. The truck cab wouldn't stop those bullets!

56

A strange sight, the raider on the hill stood up, holding his stomach, and after a couple of staggering steps, fell and did not move. The fourth rifle was a friend!

The big rifle spoke again, three quick shots, this time toward the two men behind the rocks. The two men jumped up and ran, jig jagging between rocks and bushes, disappearing down a draw. Gilbert attempted to stand and get a shot at them, but his wounded leg collapsed under him. The big rifle remained silent.

Adam watched the two men run down the draw and stood up from his hiding place almost three hundred yards down the road. Slinging his rifle over his left shoulder, he approached the man next to the truck. Gilbert was leaning on his rifle.

"Many thanks, Mister, for your timely interference. I was in well over my head." Gilbert smiled at the approaching stranger.

"Glad to help," Adam replied. "I had to wait awhile to see who the bad guys were. I couldn't tell until I heard him yell and you burst out the trailer door. That took some guts."

Adam offered his hand to Gilbert. "My name is Adam Waterman."

"Gilbert Townsend. I'm sure gl--." He was interrupted by the arrival of Emily, who flew out the door.

"Oh, thank you, Lord, for answering my prayer," Emily sobbed and threw her arms around Adam's neck. "Adam, you saved us." Emily continued to hug and kiss Adam.

Gilbert stood with his mouth agape. "You two know each other?"

"I, I--." Adam stammered, completely bewildered. Townsend! You're Emily's father!"

The flap of the big tent moved cautiously back, and Wilson, Martinez and Rusty appeared, each holding a rifle at ready.

"Boss, we thought we heard a rifle shot." Wilson spoke for the trio.

Gilbert laughed shakily. "You missed the war, men. This gentleman saved my bacon and yours. Run up on the knoll and check on Rocco. He is either dead or badly hurt."

"Check on that other guy, too please." Adam spoke over the head of Emily, who was still clinging to him.

"Now, tell me how you know my daughter, and how you happen to be here at such an opportune time." Gilbert was not a little suspicious.

"Well, I--." Adam was interrupted by Emily.

"Dad, I should have mentioned it before. I'm sorry." Emily interceded. "I met Adam, when I got into Tehachapi. Three men annoyed me in Mojave, when I stopped there for dinner. I just got up and left and apparently they followed me on to Tehachapi. Adam drove them away from the restaurant, and then we had dinner together. I didn't expect them to be so violent and so persistent."

"I am doing a survey for the U.S. Treasury Department." Adam took up the story. "I am checking all producing gold mines in southern California for their production data and estimate of their longevity. Your mine was apparently my next site as I was just following my GPS, when I came upon their parked SUV. I recognized the vehicle and tracked them on up to here on foot."

"When I heard the shooting, I waited to see who was where, before entering the fray. I'm sorry that you were hurt while I was waiting."

Marge, in the meantime, had arrived with a pan of hot water and bandages for dressing Gilbert's injured leg.

Gilbert nodded his head in agreement, his suspicions allayed. "I wouldn't want you to be shooting at my side with that weapon. Could I look at it?"

"Sure. It is just an old World War 2 infantry rifle. It is an M-One, semi-automatic. Great weapon. It is accurate to almost a half mile with a scope." Adam handed Gilbert the rifle.

"Really? That is a long ways!"

"The Marine Corps qualifies its boot camp boys at five hundred yards on a man-sized target." Adam accepted the return of his weapon.

"Boss, Rocco and another guy are up here. Both dead." Wilson called down from the knoll.

"Throw a blanket over them," Gilbert replied. "The sheriff will want to see them. I'll call him shortly."

"Wish I hadn't had to kill him." Adam's voice reflected his distaste.

ADAM AT THE MINE

Gilbert Townsend showed no sign of nervousness with the arrival of the County Sheriff and the Coroner. This was not the case with his three employees, who quickly found work to do out of sight.

The Sheriff accepted Gilbert's explanation that it was a pure case of attempted robbery and kidnapping. Adam added the name and description of Heinz Bauer and the description of the vehicle. A driver's license in the name of Jud Bauer was found on the dead man, which further substantiated their stories.

"Young lady, you were indeed fortunate that this man happened by when he did," the sheriff said to Emily. "You need to watch out for the other two. They appear to be desperate characters!"

"Surely, you will find them and arrest them, won't you, Sheriff," Emily asked nervously.

"Well, Miss, it is easy enough to lose oneself in these hills and I only have a few deputies." The sheriff defended himself.

The sheriff issued an APB (All Points Bulletin) on Bauer, using the description that Adam provided. They then loaded the two corpses into the sheriff's van and drove away.

The sigh of relief from Gilbert drew a questioning glance from Adam.

"These small town police always make me nervous," Gilbert answered Adam's look. "They are unpredictable."

"Still, the sheriff is right. The Bauers may seek revenge," Adam replied. "You are quite vulnerable here."

"We will not be caught by surprise again," Gilbert reassured him. "I'll not be without a weapon within reach. The men had grown complacent. Rocco's death was a wake-up call!"

"I don't feel right about your driving into town by yourself," Adam said to Emily. "Now that I know where to find you, I will pick you up tomorrow evening."

"Adam and I are having dinner together tomorrow, Dad," Emily explained.

"Are you sure it is safe?" Gilbert was a little dubious.

"I am always armed." Adam flipped back his jacket lapel to reveal his shoulder-holstered pistol. "While I am here, could I look at your mine? I need to fill out a form and ask a couple of questions."

"I am going to have to stay off this leg for a bit, but Emily could show you the mine," Gilbert replied. Leaning heavily on Marge, he headed for the mobile home.

"The small tent is the men's bunkhouse," Emily pointed out. "The larger one is kind of a living area, we take our meals there and it also serves to conceal the mine entrance."

The noise of the jackhammer grew louder as they approached the mouth of the mine. The generator outside the tent added to the clamor. Inside, Wilson manned the jackhammer, attacking the rock formation, Rusty was filling the Stryker.

"That is an abandoned branch." Emily shouted above the din and pointed to a second opening.

Adam noticed a small area of uncovered electric cord that seemed to lead into that opening, but thought little about it. "I understand why they didn't hear the shooting," he shouted and pointed toward the exit.

"I need to get back to my truck. I hope the Bauers didn't demo it," Adam stated as they emerged from the mine. "I'll come back and complete the form for the Treasury."

"Be careful, Adam. Those men might still be around," Emily cautioned.

Adam nodded and started back down the trail at a fast walk, the rifle held in the ready position. He circled his truck before approaching it to satisfy himself that no ambush existed. Assured that the area was clear, he walked on in and unlocked the truck door in preparation to drive back to the mine.

"Guess they were too busy making tracks out of here to look for my transportation. Still, they know what I look like and won't have any trouble finding what I drive. I must watch my back," Adam said to himself.

"I actually have just two questions for you, Mister Townsend. Approximately how much gold are you taking out per month? And what is your estimate of its longevity?" Adam had filled out the location and name of the mine (Jodie's).

"We are taking out one to two ounces per week," Gilbert said smoothly. The vein is improving slightly every week. I hope to continue another year."

"That's great news, Mister Townsend. The old records show only a fraction of that kind of production," Adam said warmly.

"Well, old Jodie was using just a hammer and chisel. It was a major effort to explore off the small vein that he was following," Gilbert excused him.

ADAM MEETS THE FAMILY

"Damn it all. They got Jud!" Heinz Bauer was gasping for breath after his run from the mine site.

"Are we just going to let them get away with that," Otto inquired angrily, also between pants.

"No, we ain't going to let them get away with anything," Heinz snarled back. "We had them cold until that stranger showed up. He was deadly with that rifle. We were lucky to see that look-out man, before he saw us."

"What are we going to do, Heinz?"

"Let me think. We know there are more than just the man and his daughter at the mine. I heard a jackhammer while we were shootin. We need to catch that girl away from there, so we will just watch. I'm going to drive on up to the main road. We will hide our car and see if anyone comes back up the trail."

The two men had waited over an hour before they heard Adam's pickup and saw his dust. Well hidden in a clump of shrubs, they were unseen by Adam as he pulled onto the main road. Recognizing Adam from their encounter at the restaurant, they had the identity of the rifleman and his transportation.

Heinz Bauer almost grinned. "Maybe we can kill three birds with one stone."

Adam was a bit disappointed not to have been invited to lunch by the Townsends. Emily's Dad didn't seem to be anxious for me to hang around. Maybe he has doubts about a guy that is too handy with guns, paying attention to his daughter. Well, the food at the restaurant isn't too bad. Maybe I can get another mine checked out this afternoon. I should call Captain Walker and report this episode to him, in case there are some repercussions.

It was still sunny when Adam returned to the mine to pick up his date for the evening. Emily had apparently been waiting, as she was out the door and to his truck before Adam could get out. She let herself into the cab.

"So glad to see you, Adam. I have been so restless today. Seems like I am afraid to be out of your sight now. Guess I got too wound up yesterday." Emily reached over and squeezed Adam's arm.

"I've been pretty jumpy today, also," Adam admitted. "I would feel a lot better if I knew where those two goons are. Maybe the sheriff's APB will turn up something."

"Well, let's forget them tonight. What do you have planned, Adam?"

"I was told about an old restaurant down town that has a large model train set that simulates the one into Tehachapi from Bakersfield. The train actually does a full circle, crossing over itself to gain enough altitude to clear the mountains," Adam enthused. "They said the food is excellent, they also have a dance band in a hall adjoining it on Saturday nights."

"That sounds lovely, Adam. I love to dance."

Adam seemed to enjoy the model train more than Emily, but both greeted the prime rib dinner special with enthusiasm. Adam, a mediocre dancer, seemed to excel with Emily in his arms

They were almost the only couple left at midnight when the band played "Goodnight, Sweetheart" and began to put away their instruments. Reluctantly, Adam escorted Emily back to his truck for the trip back to the mine.

"Adam, are you attending church tomorrow," Emily asked hesitantly.

"Actually, yes. There is a small church at the edge of town, called 'The Shepherd of the Hills'. I attended there once before. Would you like to go with me?"

"Would you mind? My parents aren't into church and I feel the need for some spiritual guidance. My life is in turmoil, what with college, those men and you, Adam." The darkness hid the tears in Emily's eyes.

Their goodnight kiss was longer than either of them expected. Finally, Emily broke away.

"Thank you for the nicest evening that I have ever had, Adam."

Adam drove back to town with his heart singing. "Lord, please make this lovely creature my mate. You know, Lord, I have been searching a long time and never before has any girl seemed right. Please make it so!"

It was a small church with an even smaller congregation. The young pastor, obviously his first church, bubbled over with enthusiasm.

"In my opinion, Psalms is the most beautiful book in the Bible. High on the list of fine passages in Psalms is chapter 121. I will give you a minute to find it. Now read with me: I WILL LIFT MY EYES UNTO THE HILLS. WHERE DOES MY HELP COME FROM? MY HELP COMES FROM THE LORD, MAKER OF HEAVEN AND EARTH! HE WILL NOT LET YOUR FOOT SLIP. HE, WHO WATCHES OVER YOU, WILL NOT SLUMBER."

"There it is in a nutshell, folks. You put your trust in the Lord and he will take care of you. David wrote a whole bunch of the Book of Psalms. Here is what he said in Psalms 30. I WILL EXALT YOU, O LORD, FOR YOU LIFTED ME OUT OF THE DEPTHS AND DID NOT LET MY ENEMIES GLOAT OVER ME. O LORD, MY GOD, I CALLED TO YOU FOR HELP AND YOU HEALED ME."

"Even though David had many, many successes, he also spent a lot of time fleeing for his life. King Saul, whom David served so faithfully, tried to kill him when he felt David was vying for the throne. David's eldest son, his first-born, wanted his father's throne and chased after him to kill him. How terrible! His own son, so enamored with being king that he would kill his own father to get it."

"Even though David was a great man, blessed by the Lord, he wasn't a perfect man. He drifted into adultery and later arranged for the killing of the woman's husband to cover up his misdeeds. But, he pleased God, when he repented, fell to his knees and asked for forgiveness."

"God will be pleased with us imperfect men, if we, instead of standing up like a man, will fall on our knees like a man, like David, and pray for help. Lift your eyes to the hills that surround us and ask for the help that the Lord is waiting to give us."

"Now I know some of you have troubles and tribulations that you are trying to deal with on your own. Swallow your pride and come forward to the altar and lay them on Jesus' shoulders."

As the organ played "Do Not Pass Me By", several rose from their seat and went forward; among them was Emily Townsend.

"I'm not sure I want Emily running around with this Adam Waterman," Gilbert growled to his wife. "And going to church! Where did that come from, college?"

It was Sunday morning and Emily had just left with Adam.

"I don't know, Gil. Adam seems very nice," Marge replied. "He did practically save our lives."

"It's that pistol that he carries. Why would a data collector from the Treasury Department have a permit to carry a gun? It is a thirty-eight caliber special. A lot of the police departments like them." Gilbert looked thoughtful.

THE BAUERS

The two men pored over a large topographical map of the Tehachapi area.

"We gotta find a place to hide out. Those damned cops will be looking for us," the older man cursed.

"Heinz, why don't we just forget that girl, and go on to Bakersfield, like we planned? We got nothin except trouble here," Otto whined.

"No way! They killed Jud, and that chick is going to pay and her boyfriend, too," Heinz snarled. "There is an old abandoned mine off this trail, but our SUV wouldn't make it."

"We could steal a jeep, Heinz." Otto finally gave in. "We could watch for one at the motel."

The black SUV had been parked in the remote corner of the motel parking lot for a couple hours. It was full dark now. They had been parked there to pick up a jeep. Their target was a tan Jeep Wrangler that a young couple had driven into the motel, and they were in now their motel suite. Heinz was waiting until their lights were extinguished.

"There! They're in bed. Get the jeep door open, while I get the license tags off that Buick," Heinz whispered.

An old couple had driven the Buick in. Heinz wanted their license plates to put on the jeep. He didn't think they would notice that their plates were missing.

Otto jumped from the SUV with a door jimmy in his hands. In minutes, he was crouched under the dashboard of the jeep, hot-wiring the ignition. And a few minutes later, the jeep idled out of its parking spot and pulled onto the highway. The black SUV followed.

The two vehicles proceeded to a side street in town, there the two thieves transferred all their gear from the SUV to the Wrangler. Heinz printed 'FUEL PUMP BUSTED. WAITING FOR PARTS', on a sheet of paper and laid it on the dash. Leaving the SUV parked, they both entered the jeep and drove away.

66

The trail showed evidence of recent use, but no tire tracks showed up in front of the abandoned mine where he was searching. However, animal tracks led into the mine entrance.

"Otto, grab your carbine and see if anyone is around the mine," Heinz instructed. "Take the flashlight."

Otto reluctantly slid out of the jeep, clutching his small rifle and warily made his way to the mine entrance. He disappeared shortly, as he swept the light beam around the interior of the mine. He was greeted by a loud snarl as a giant cat burst by him.

Otto fell backward with a scream of terror

Heinz burst out laughing as Otto climbed to his feet. "Don't think that cougar appreciated having his siesta disturbed."

"I don't see anything funny," Otto growled as he climbed back into the jeep. "Here's the flashlight. You do the inspection and I'll hold down the front seat."

Chuckling, Heinz took the flashlight and his carbine and entered the mine.

"This is fine. Can even back the jeep in almost completely out of sight," Heinz commented as he returned. "We'll unload our gear and you go back to that little 'Stop and Go' on the west edge of town. Get us some grub and a case of drinking water. No booze! I'll scout around for a spring of water and what else I can find. Don't forget to put on those Buick license plates."

"I need some money, Heinz."

After Otto had driven away, Heinz spotted the remnants of an old footpath, leading off to the south. He followed it for almost a quarter mile before espying a green area. It proved to be a small stream of water, seeping out of a hillside. Someone had dug a shallow hole and lined it with stones. Tracks of many birds and animals proved that it was well used. One set of large paw tracks covered the others.

"Reckon Otto's cougar friend stopped here." Heinz grinned at the thought of his brother's scare.

He dipped his hand in the water and took a sip. He wrinkled his nose, the water was highly alkaline.

"Reckon it will do except for drinking. We'll stick to bottled water for that."

As Heinz began to retrace his steps back to the mine, he stopped and gazed out to the east.

Old Jodie's mine is out this way. That's where our girl friend is. Wonder if I can walk there from here? Need to look at that map again.

He hurried back to the mine with new energy. Retrieving the map, he searched for the mark he had made earlier.

"Here it is. Couldn't be more than five miles, straight as the crow flies," he muttered to himself. "It's only ten-thirty. I'll grab a couple of trail bars and fill a canteen with that spring water. I'll do it!"

After leaving a note for Otto that he was "visiting their girlfriend", Heinz struck out with the map folded and his route marked in red.

Being adept at reading a map, Heinz had no difficulty following the route to Gilbert's mine. Even arriving from another direction, it was easy to recognize the knoll where they maintained a lookout man.

"That guy is wide awake. Gotta be careful."

Circling around to a point opposite the lookout to another high point, where he could observe the encampment, Heinz settled down to watch. Soon he saw a redheaded man come from the larger tent with a rifle in his hand. The redhead climbed the knoll and the other man descended and reentered the tent.

Aha! There are at least two more guys here beside the old man. We were lucky the other day. We could have stirred up a bee's nest. Those are AK-15s those guys are carrying. A lot of firepower. I wonder if they keep a lookout man at night. I would like to get close enough to hear and see who all is living here.

Heinz ate another trail bar, had a drink of the spring water, and set back to wait for sunset. It was warm under the partial shade of the clump of bushes that hid him and he fought dozing off. The short night of sleep after stealing the jeep didn't help.

Something jarred him awake in time to see the redhead descending the knoll and entering the tent. The sun was below the horizon. A middle-aged woman emerged from the travel trailer with an armload of food. The girl and a young Mexican followed, equally laden. They entered the larger tent. Must be supper time. It suddenly occurred to Heinz that the truck that the old man drove was absent. Heinz checked his watch.

"We'll come back tomorrow night with my moccasins, and I'll sneak down and listen. The old guy will probably be back then."

Heinz slipped back out of sight and made his way back to his new quarters.

Otto was pacing nervously in front of the mine. He had a small fire burning and it developed that he was more concerned that the cougar would return than that of Heinz's wellbeing.

Heinz scoffed at his fears and cussed him out for not having fixed any supper. He opened a can of pork and beans and devoured the contents, while relating his experiences to his brother. He, then blew up his air mattress, unrolled his bedroll and went to sleep. Otto chose to sleep in the back seat of the Wrangler.

Sunset the following night found the two Bauers looking down on Gilbert Townsend's camp. They recognized Gilbert's truck parked by the trailer. The sound of an approaching vehicle made them duck down out of sight. A four-wheel drive pick-up carrying a Quad pulled into the parking area.

"That's the guy that drove us out of the restaurant," Otto exclaimed excitedly. "Let's kill him!"

"Shut up, you fool. We'd have the whole outfit to fight. We ain't ready," Heinz replied disgustedly.

Emily rushed out of the trailer, climbed into the pick-up and they drove away.

The two men watched the lookout man descend from the knoll and the lights come on in the big tent. Again, food was brought from the trailer, borne by Gilbert, Marge and Martinez. As they disappeared inside, the two men crept down from the hill to noiselessly sidle up next to the tent.

At first there was little conversation, as everyone hungrily attacked the food, then one of the men cleared his throat.

"Boss, we were wondering. With Rocco gone, it's hard to keep up and stand guard, too."

"We thought maybe the girl could help," another voice added.

"No way!" Gilbert's authoritative voice was unmistakable. "Emily must know nothing about our operation. I'll kill anyone that breathes a hint to her. Martinez can quit helping Marge in the kitchen, I will take a turn on guard duty, when I am here."

"Rocco never did anything with his checks, Boss," the first voice persisted. "They are still in his duffel bag. How do we split them up?"

We split his total share equally, five ways. Sound fair to you guys?" It was a question, but Gilbert's voice indicated it was final.

"Sure, Boss. Sounds good to me," the first voice replied, followed by affirmatives from the others.

Heinz looked at Otto in surprise and motioned for them to return to the hill. They carefully withdrew.

"What were they talking about, Heinz," Otto asked, when they were a safe distance away.

"Shut up and let me think," Heinz snapped. "Let's go back to camp."

Their return trip was in darkness and there was no conversation as they groped their way. Even with flashlights, it was difficult to find the right direction.

It was almost midnight when they arrived. Heinz immediately ordered Otto to fix some food. Otto lit the propane camp stove and put on some sliced ham.

"Uh, Heinz. I bought a bottle. Do you want some," Otto asked hesitantly.

"Bring it out," Heinz directed, apparently forgetting his order, not to buy any booze.

"Why is their operation so important that he don't want his girl to find out? Ain't they just mining for gold," Heinz mused. "And split the dead man's checks? They ain't been hauling out that much gold. Something else is going on there. I need to watch them; see if I can learn something."

Heinz slammed his fist on his knee!

"It has something to do with the old man's trips. He was all loaded to go somewhere, the other morning, when we attacked them.

"Otto, get some sleep and drive the Wrangler over to, where his trail hits the main road. Stay out of sight, I'll go back there at sun-up and call you if the old man leaves with his truck," Heinz directed. "Be careful not to let him see you, but follow him and find out where he goes."

The sky was beginning to lighten when Heinz regained his position to spy down on Gilbert's mine encampment. A man emerged from the smaller tent, yawning with rifle in hand, climbed to their usual look out post. The now familiar routine of bringing food from the trailer house to the main tent followed, except for the girl climbing the knoll with a plate of food for the lookout man.

Heinz's stomach growled, as the smell of fried bacon drifted up to him. Stoically, he waited with his eyes glued to the tent opening. Finally, the men emerged carrying sacks of ore. Disgusted, Heinz backed away from the brow of the hill and dialed Otto.

"Forget it. He's just taking some ore to the assay office in Tehachapi. Go on back to the mine. I'll see you there."

Heinz made his way off the hill and back to the mine, where Otto had breakfast waiting for him. He would try again tomorrow.

THE HIDEOUT

Adam had only a few sites on the map to check out. His vision of locating the crooks hiding out in an abandoned mine and converting the gold bars into cash was growing dim. Also in the picture now, was his attraction for Emily Townsend.

He did not want to go back to Los Angeles and not see her anymore, but could not justify staying around Tehachapi much longer. He contemplated taking vacation time and even leaving the Police Department. Something kept him from proposing marriage to her, even though she seemed to share his attraction.

He finally decided to talk to Captain Walker, lay it all out on the table, and ask for his advice. He took out his cell phone to call.

"On second thought, I think I will wait until I am completely finished with the gold mining sites before I talk to him," he muttered to himself and replaced his phone. "I can hit another one today."

Adam decided to visit a site that he had been avoiding due to the rough terrain. The trail looked too rough for his truck and he reasoned that transporting the gold would be prohibitive.

"Maybe they are counting on that. I need to check it out, anyhow," he mused. "I'll leave the truck at the motel and just drive the Quad."

As Adam turned off the main road onto the dirt road, he noticed several sets of tire tracks, but disregarded that as there were a couple of residences in that direction. Some of the tracks turned off further on. Consulting his map, he saw a particular steep gully ahead. The GPS indicated it was still a couple miles from the old mine site.

"Think I will just walk on in. It gives me a chance to hunt for rocks. I'll hide the Quad. Better carry my rifle though."

As Adam walked along the trail, he noted that the trail had gone unused for a long while, but showed several recent trips. The steep area would not have been any trouble for the Quad, however, the vehicle preceding him had some difficulty.

71

"That's odd. No traffic for a long time and all of a sudden a bunch of traffic. Maybe I should walk a little softer. I may have stumbled onto something!" Adam slid his rifle off his shoulder and walked with it "at ready", his interest in rocks disappeared.

He moved off the trail to consult his topographical map. "Another quarter mile looks like. I need to stay off the soft dirt. Best I leave no tracks. I'll just stay off the trail entirely."

Moving from bush to bush and crouching down as best he could to avoid detection, Adam advanced onto the mine site. For several minutes he hid, watching for any activity. All was quiet.

"No vehicle in sight. It was probably a jeep. It wouldn't carry much gold at a time."

He cut a heavy branch from the bush he was hiding behind and advanced cautiously to the mouth of the mine. He would use the branch to brush out his footprints.

"Fair sized mine. Two sleeping bags. No sign of any gold. Darn! I was hoping. Looks like two guys hiding out. Wait a minute! Could this be the Bauers? They would never get their SUV over that trail. Could have owned another vehicle though. Best I get myself away from here before somebody comes back, just in case."

Adam carefully erased his footprints with the branch as he retreated to the bushes. Safely out of sight, he called the local sheriff's department. The receptionist agreed to have the sheriff call him back when he was free.

Adam made his way back to the Quad and drove back to the motel. It was still mid-afternoon, his experience that day convinced him to call Captain Walker right then.

"Detective Waterman, I'm glad you called. I have some info for you, but tell me why you called," Captain Walker answered the phone.

"Captain, I have had zero results in my search for the ransom gold crooks. I only have a couple left to check. The thing is, I am mixed up in another situation. I have been seeing a young lady on a regular basis the past few weeks." Adam went on to relate how he met Emily, and their mix-up with the Bauers.

"Does the local sheriff know that you are a United States Deputy Marshall, Adam?"

"No, Sir. I haven't told him. I was afraid my real mission there would be compromised," Adam replied.

72

"Whether or not you reveal your search for the ransom parties, I leave to your judgment, but you definitely should let him know that you are an officer of the law. Especially if you have 'perps' gunning for you and you have eliminated one of them," Captain Walker persisted.

"I'll do that, Sir, there's something else, too. I have learned to care a lot about this girl and I don't trust the local authorities to protect her. I can't honestly stay here after I finish checking the old mines. I am thinking about taking some vacation time."

"I see what you mean. Let me think, have the sheriff request your assistance from the Federal Marshall. You can add your endorsement. He will probably authorize it and pick up the tab. Be good advertising for him." Captain Walker chuckled.

"If that takes care of your questions, I have some information for you. As you know, the Treasury keeps a log on all raw gold transactions over five thousand dollars. We asked to be notified of any sudden increase from any source. I got several notifications. One from the Reno Gold Refinery reported a reopening of an old mine near there that has brought in over four million in the last month. Thought you would want to check it out. I will text you the coordinates."

"Four million in four weeks is a bunch of gold," Adam exclaimed. "This could be the break we are looking for. If it is in Nevada, I could get the FBI back on the case."

"Keep me informed, Waterman." Captain Walker rang off.

"Whoa! Four million, a million per week. That has to be them; they will have all the gold exchanged for cash in a couple years. I have to get over there. Yeah! Here's the Captain's text. With a little help from my GPS, it's a done deal," Adam exulted.

"I can't leave Emily alone. Maybe she will go with me. I'll call her. Also need to call the sheriff, but Emily first."

Adam's cell phone rang as he was about to dial. It was the sheriff returning his call. Adam told him about the campsite at the old mine.

"It is off "Whiskey Trail", the map calls it," Adam explained.

"I know the place," the sheriff replied. "Used to have trouble with kids partying out there until a cougar gave some of them a bad scare. You think the Bauers might be hid out there?"

"Well, it fits. Only thing, they drive a SUV, which couldn't get there on that trail," Adam responded.

"I'll check it out tomorrow, anyhow. I appreciate the tip, Waterman."

"You're welcome. Sheriff, there is something else I need to tell you. Besides working for the U.S. Treasury, I am also a Federal Deputy Marshall. Should you feel the need for some help with the Bauers, a letter to my bosses would allow me to help you."

"So you're a lawman. Well, I'm not surprised. I'll send out the letter and I will welcome all the assistance I can get."

Adam's next call was to Emily.

"Hi Emily. I need to talk to you. Could you have dinner with me tonight?"

"I'd love to, Adam. I could drive in."

"No way! I don't want you going anywhere by yourself while the Bauers are around. I will pick you up at six-thirty," Adam exclaimed.

"I'll be waiting, Adam. Thank you."

Although Emily was burning up with curiosity, she refrained from asking any questions until Adam had ordered the wine.

"All right, Adam. You have my undivided attention. What do we need to talk about?"

"Well, we could discuss how extra ordinarily beautiful you are tonight," Adam teased.

"Now that is music to my ears and I'll not cease enjoying that music, especially from you," Emily retorted, "but I doubt if that is to be our main topic."

"I need to drive over to Nevada to check out a gold mine. I don't want to leave you here. I want you to go with me," Adam said seriously. "We could spend the night in Reno and take in a show."

"No hanky-panky," Emily stated firmly.

"No hanky-panky," Adam reiterated. "We get separate rooms."

"Then I'll do it! Oh, Adam, I have never been to Reno. It will be great fun. I don't want to gamble, but they have some great shows there." Emily was almost bouncing in her chair.

"I thought we would spend two nights there and drive back through Yosemite National Forest," Adam added with a grin. "It is a beautiful drive through the mountains. We may have to spend another night as it is slow driving."

"Oh, I am so excited, I don't think I'll be able to eat dinner," Emily bubbled.

"Maybe we should just skip dinner and start out now," Adam chuckled.

"No, no. I have to pack. Oh, I don't have a thing to wear. Adam, what do people wear there to see the shows," Emily worried.

"I think they are about as casual as main street of Tehachapi on Saturday morning." Adam continued to chuckle at Emily's reaction.

'No need to tell her about those two goons camping out near here. It would just dampen her fun.'

"When are we leaving?" Emily inquired. "I need to get ready,"

"I will be at your door promptly at six thirty in the morning, day after tomorrow. You will have precisely ten minutes to load your stuff. We will eat breakfast on down the road." Adam kept a stern face for that ultimatum.

Their dinner order arrived at that moment to defer any more discussion. In spite of her earlier declaration, Emily made short work of her chicken fried steak.

As promised, Adam was in front of the trailer house promptly at the appointed time. Emily had apparently taken his ultimatum seriously, as she was out the door with suitcase in hand, before Adam's truck came to a stop. Adam drew her to him for a long kiss before opening the truck door for her. This would be a momentous trip for him!

RENO

Wearily the two tired travelers climbed from the truck. It had been a long drive with only two stops, one for breakfast and the other for gas and lunch. Adam had called ahead for reservations, so in short order they were signed in for their rooms.

"Give me thirty minutes for a shower and I am ready for dinner," Emily chirped. "I'm starved."

Slot machines lined the lobby with an occasional player. A large poster advertised the current dinner show. Emily was ecstatic.

"Adam, look. April Showers is performing tonight. I just love her. She has a truly golden voice."

"Great! She comes on in forty-five minutes. We're just in time," Adam responded.

The dining room was not crowded and they were shown to a table immediately. The waiters were rushing to get all the orders in and filled before the performance began. Adam and Emily obliged by ordering two rib eye steaks and their waiter rushed away.

In her mid-thirties, Ms Showers had lost her girlish figure, but her voice had only grown stronger. Her all-white maxi skirt and blouse set off her dark hair. A single strand of black pearls and black pearl earrings was her only jewelry.

"Those of you that know me, know that I like to sprinkle some Christian music into my shows," she announced in a rich contralto voice. "I know this offends some people and I am truly sorry. My opening number is "Holy Spirit, You are Welcome in This Place".

Only a muted trumpet accompanied her as she sang, repeating the words three times. A period of intense quiet followed the last notes of her song, and then people began standing and clapping.

Emily caught a tear trickling down her cheek. "Thank you, Adam for bringing me here."

The rest of the show was a mixture of modern, oldies and Christian music. That the show was a success was indicated by the many standing ovations. She closed with "How Great Thou Art". The lights slowly dimmed as she ended. When the lights came back up, the stage was empty. The entire dining room stood and clapped until April Showers reappeared.

"Can we leave now, Adam? She just drains me emotionally, and it has been a tiring drive," Emily whispered.

"Of course, Emily. Get some sleep. Sleep in if you like, or we could meet for breakfast," Adam responded.

"No, please call me when you are awake. I want to meet you for breakfast.

They made their way back to their rooms.

"Emily, I need to take care of some business this morning. You are going to have to entertain yourself for a while."

They were finishing breakfast at the hotel diner.

"Can't I go with you, Adam? I will just sit quietly in the car."

"Out of the question, Honey. I probably will be riding the Quad most of the time, as the mine is rather far out." Adam looked sideways at his breakfast partner, but she appeared not to notice his pet name. "I am told a woman can always go shopping."

"Yes, but I would rather be with you," Emily responded.

"Maybe we should figure out a way where you could spend full time with me," Adam grinned.

"Adam Waterman, are you proposing to me?" Emily flashed him a startled look.

"Well, I was hoping for a little more romantic atmosphere, but now that you mention it, yes I am. I love you, Emily. Will you marry me?"

Emily's delighted laugh drew the attention of the couple in the next table.

"Then I accept your proposal. I would love to marry you, Adam Waterman."

"Really? You will?" Adam sprang to his feet. "Hey everybody. She's going to marry me!"

The tables around him cheered and clapped.

Emily, red in the face now, whispered," Adam, you dofus! Sit down."

Adam chuckled as he regained his seat. "This isn't really an engagement ring, but the Post Office finally tracked me down yesterday."

Adam pulled a small box from his coat pocket and handed it to Emily, who immediately opened it. Inside was a pair of agate earrings, set in silver and custom made from the stones, which he had shown her on their first date.

"They are beautiful, Adam! Oh, thank you." Emily pulled Adam's head to her and gave him a kiss.

Reluctantly Adam rose to his feet. "I have to leave now. I will try to get back as soon as possible. Maybe you can look at engagement rings," he chuckled.

"I'll be fine, Darling. I'll sit here and have another cup of coffee and admire my new earrings," Emily responded and held her face up for a good-bye kiss.

Adam returned to his room and changed into a camouflage outfit, complete with shoulder holster, pistol and rifle. He carried an ammunition belt over his right shoulder as he strode out to his truck. He hoped he was ready for whatever awaited him at the mine.

Following his GPS, Adam drove back the way he had come for several miles before turning off on a country road. The road was dusty and well traveled. The GPS showed twelve miles to his destination. After six miles, the road suddenly deteriorated to just a beaten trail with very little signs of traffic. Soon further travel was impossible for his truck.

"No working mine using this trail," Adam muttered to himself as he unloaded his Quad. "They could have another way in though."

Relieved of the weight of the Quad, Adam was able to turn the truck around to point back down the trail before proceeding on his Quad. He saw an occasional broken brush that indicated a vehicle had been through here, but several weeks ago. With a mile yet to go, Adam elected to park and go the rest of the way on foot.

No use advertising my approach, in case the occupants aren't friendly.

A large pile of rock and debris alerted Adam that he had arrived. Dry weeds decorated the pile. It had been a long time since anything had been added to the pile. An aura of desolation pervaded the area. Adam relaxed his vigilance, but still carried the rifle at a ready position.

He entered the mine, quickly stepping to one side and sweeping the interior with his flashlight. The excavation was empty, but had had extensive working at one time. That it was heavily visited by wildlife now was evident by the tracks in the dusty floor. Here and there, a man's boot track showed. At one time, the mine had been visited by a person, how long ago Adam could only guess.

"There wasn't any four million in gold taken out of here last month," Adam said to himself in disgust.

He checked his cell phone for reception. It showed only one bar. He might be able to dial out. His call to his captain drew an answering machine. The broken message indicated he was out for lunch.

"Figures. I wouldn't be able to communicate, even if he would have answered."

Adam slung his rifle on his shoulder and headed back for his Quad.

It was mid-afternoon when Adam drove up to his hotel. He had eaten a couple of trail bars from his stash in the truck, so felt able to wait until dinnertime to eat again. A check of Emily's room was negative. She was still shopping.

He called Captain Walker and related his experience at the mine. "I'm guessing that someone checked it out and is just using it to satisfy the requirements. The gold is obviously coming from elsewhere."

"Well, you are out of my jurisdiction now," the captain chuckled. "But if I were you, I would ease down to the Reno Refinery and ask some questions. If it is our ransom gold coming in, they will send another shipment shortly. Maybe they can get a description, or even a photograph of the ones bringing it in."

"I'll do that, Captain."

A light tap on the door alerted Adam that Emily was probably finished with her shopping for the day.

"Someone at the door, Captain. I will stay in touch." Adam hung up.

"Come in," he called. "It's unlocked."

Emily burst in the door, several bags clutched in her left hand.

"Oh good. You're back. I'm starved, could we eat an early dinner?"

Adam spread his hands, indicating his grubby condition. "If you want to go with me looking this way, we can leave now."

"Nooo! I'm not that starved. Besides, I'm all hot and sweaty. Can we leave in about an hour? The Golden Nugget has a special on prime ribs."

"I'll come a-knockin at your door," Adam sing-songed as Emily let herself out.

"Adam, bring the stones that you showed me that first night, please."

They were sitting in the dining room, sipping wine. Emily was wearing a new skirt and blouse that she had found in a "fabulous sale" and showing off her new earrings.

"I did look at some jewelry, some engagement rings," Emily admitted hesitantly. "I think I know what I want for an engagement ring. Did you bring your gems with you? Good." As Adam produced a handful of stones. "That blue one. I think you said it was the official California gem.

"A benitoite." Adam supplied.

"Yes, that's it." Emily held up the light blue gem. "Could you have it cut and set in gold with a diamond chip on each side of it?"

"I'm sure I could, if that is what you want. Chin Li is very creative. Draw him a picture to work on. It so happens that he has a larger stone than this of mine. I'll have him use that one."

"Now that's settled, we need to order," Adam directed. "You might be able to live on love, but I need some prime rib."

After dinner, Adam gave Emily five dollars in quarters. She was elated when her last quarter hit a six-dollar jackpot. Adam pretended to be upset that he hadn't given her silver dollars instead.

They found a musical revue, which they enjoyed. Emily made Adam cover his eyes when scantily clad ladies came on. It was a good evening.

On the way out of town the next morning, Adam stopped at the Reno Refinery and presented his credentials.

He found that the owner of the mine that he was investigating had been in the day before with over two million in gold quartz. They promised to pay special attention to the carrier on his next visit.

Adam and Emily had a delightful drive back to Tehachapi.

ROBBERS ROBBED

The two Bauer's had left their hideout at dawn. Otto took the jeep to park and wait at the intersection of the main road and the trail to the Townsend mine. His assignment was to follow Gilbert Townsend, if Heinz thought he was taking gold to other than the local assay office.

Heinz had hiked over the hills, directly to the Townsend mine to observe the loading of Gilbert's truck.

Both of the Bauers were absent, when the sheriff descended on their lair with two deputies. Each of the three sheriffs were carrying twelve-gauge shotguns, besides their regular side arms. They paused behind the pile of rock and debris.

"Hey, you inside. This is the county sheriff speaking. Come out with your hands empty," the sheriff called out.

They waited for several minutes before the sheriff called again, repeating his previous instructions. He then sent one of the deputies forward to inspect, while they stood ready with their shotguns.

"No one here, Sheriff," the deputy called back, after looking in the mine entrance.

The other two moved forward now and the sheriff looked around.

"I have no reason to search the place," the sheriff remarked. "We will check it out some evening."

They proceeded back to where they had left their vehicle.

Heinz watched as Gilbert backed his truck up to the big tent. The men carried bucket after bucket out and stacked them in the truck, until the bed was full. Gilbert, carrying his rifle, now, walked back to the trailer.

Heinz eased back out of sight and dialed his brother.

"Otto, his truck will be coming out, shortly, find out where he goes. Call me when you know something."

Someway, I got to find out what is going on in that mine. I am going to come back tonight and look. Hafta be careful, but it's the only way!

Satisfied that there was nothing more to learn from watching the campsite, Heinz crept back and headed for his own camp. At the entrance to his mine, he noticed footprints in the dirt. He back tracked them to behind the pile of debris and saw an imprint of a rifle butt in the dust.

"Aha! They were armed," he muttered. "I wonder if it was the Law. They must be looking for me and Otto. There was nothing to identify me here. Maybe they will let it go, now."

Heinz spent the day napping and cleaning his weapons. At dusk, dressed in dark clothing and carrying a pistol and two small flashlights, he headed back for the Townsend mine.

He waited patiently while the Townsends finished dinner and the lights were extinguished. It was another hour before he ventured down to the main tent. Carefully he eased behind the big tent to the mouth of the mine. With a pistol in his right hand and a small Led flashlight in the other, he stepped into the mine.

"They got all the fancy tools to mine with; jackhammer and Stryker rock crusher. Wonder why he would crush the ore instead of just taking it to the assay office in sacks. There must be something special to make him crush the rocks and haul it somewhere else. He must be hauling it a long ways as Otto hasn't called yet. Hope he didn't stop and start drinking somewhere. Damn fool!"

Heinz examined the rocks that were loose by the jackhammer without discovering any great amount of gold. The Stryker was empty and offered no clues. The sign on the branch of the excavation warned of dangerous cave-ins and Heinz started to pass that up and leave.

"Damn! Nothin here to warrant grinding up the rock ore. Wait! Is that an extension cord? Looks like it leads to that branch."

Heinz cautiously stepped into the forbidden area, flashing his light around. He gaped as the grinder came into view. He moved closer to examine it and tripped over a small pail. A dull glitter shone from the bucket as his flashlight hit it. He reached down and his fingers found the pail was full of small bars of metal. He lifted one bar up for a closer look. Gold!

A matching pail was setting a couple feet away from the first, as if a person had carried in both of them and set them down next to the grinder. The grinder wheel also glittered from flicks of pure gold. Heinz solved the problem immediately.

"They are grinding up gold bars and mixing it with sand and gravel, to simulate new gold ore, turning stolen bars into legitiment cash!. That's what he hauled away this morning."

Heinz slid the gold bar that he was holding into a pocket of his pants. He then removed three more bars from each of the pails and stuffed them into his pocket also. With his pistol gripped tightly in his hand, Heinz stepped out of the mine and by the tent. He breathed a sigh of relief as he finally reached the hilltop over looking the camp. He removed his cell phone and dialed Otto.

"Otto, where are you?"

"I'm just north of Phoenix, Heinz, and I can't hardly stay awake any longer," Otto responded.

"Just pull over and take a nap and get back here as soon as possible. I need the car."

"What's goin on, Heinz," Otto inquired curiously.

"Never mind. Get your nap, then get your butt back here."

It was close to noon the following day, when Otto drove in. Heinz was waiting impatiently for him.

"What took you so long," Heinz growled as Otto climbed stiffly from the jeep.

"It was a long trip," Otto whined. I only slept three hours, didn't even stop for breakfast. I'm tired and hungry. Don't give me no heat."

"Wait until you see what I found! You'll forget about food and sleep," Heinz said proudly, as he led the way to the mine entrance.

"There! Look at that," he showed Otto the seven gold bars, laid out on his bedroll.

"Whoa! Are those gold?" Otto's fatigue was forgotten. "Where did they come from?"

"I snagged them from old Jodie's gold mine last night, while they were sleeping," Heinz bragged.

"You mean they are making gold bars from the quartz over there," Otto gaped.

"No, you fool! They're making gold dust from the gold bars," Heinz snarled.

"Why would they do that, Heinz?" Otto was completely perplexed.

"They stole some gold bullion and can't sell it, so they are reducing the bars to gold dust and selling it to refineries for cash." Heinz curbed his impatience to explain. "Real clever, but I know where I can sell the bars. Won't get full price, but it will be fast. Grab a handful of trail bars, we are going to Bakersfield."

The pawnshop that Heinz was looking for was in the seedy part of town on a side street. Heinz made several wrong turns before he found it. He had the gold bars tucked into the side pockets of a heavy jacket, which he carried, as he pushed open the door to the shop.

"Hello, Bauer. Haven't seen you in a while. You been in jail?" The tall thin proprietor greeted them. His rather prominent hooknose supported a pair of dark glasses.

"No, I ain't been in jail, Jethro, you old skinflint," Heinz growled. "Get this business over with, our business is in the back room." He indicated an older teenager who was fidgeting at the counter.

Jethro turned back to his teenage customer. "That's the best I can do, kid. I got sacks full of gold earrings that I can't put in my showroom."

The teenager sullenly accepted the money offered and slammed out the door.

"Damn kids!" Jethro cast a contemptuous glance at the departing figure. "Rip off a house two blocks away and expect to get top dollar for them!" He returned his attention to Heinz. "You look like you swallowed the canary, show me what you are so proud of."

He led the way into a back room. The room contained half dozen chairs and a table with some jewelry tools and a set of scales. He motioned for them to take a seat. Otto took a chair, but Heinz remained standing and laid a gold bar on the table in front of Jethro. Jethro showed no sign of surprise or pleasure. He just picked up the bar and scratched it with a fingernail. Satisfied that it was pure gold, he put it on the scales.

"Ten ounces," he remarked as he returned the bar to the table.

"How much," Heinz asked impatiently.

"I could go as high as fifteen hundred," Jethro replied after a short pause.

"Why you cheap crook! That bar is worth fourteen thousand dollars and you want to buy it for a measly fifteen hundred," Heinz exploded. "I got seven of them and I can get a dozen more! If you don't want them, I'll find another buyer."

84

"Now, don't get excited, Bauer. You say you have seven? Maybe I can do a little better," Jethro soothed.

"I want ten thousand apiece," Heinz declared forcibly.

"You know I can't pay that much. That's a US Treasury bar. It has to be hotter than an oven," Jethro responded.

"Alright." Heinz cooled noticeably. "I'll take eight thousand."

"Seven thousand apiece if they are all ten ounce. That's my top dollar, or take them somewhere else! I'll write you a check."

"Forty nine thousand cash and you have a deal." Heinz laid the other six bars on the table.

Jethro rose from his chair and disappeared in the next room. He was gone several minutes and Heinz began to fidget. Finally, Jethro reappeared with a handful of money. Carefully, he counted out each bill and Heinz inspected each one to check for counterfeit. At last, Heinz was satisfied, tucked the money in the old coat pockets and they got up to leave.

Heinz wore a broad grin as they walked to the jeep. Otto was in complete shock. "Not a bad evening's work," Heinz crowed. "Let's get back to camp. I want to pick up another four bars while the old man is away."

It was dusk when the two brothers arrived at the mine again. Heinz elected to drive the jeep as far as the spring to save walking. Leaving the jeep parked, they hiked on to the Townsend mine.

"I'm leavin my rifle with you," Heinz told his brother when they arrived on the knoll overlooking the camp. "If you hear anything behind the big tent empty your gun into the smaller tent. That's where the men are sleeping."

When the lights were all out and the camp was quiet, Heinz ventured off the knoll and behind the big tent. He found the two buckets as he had left them. Without hesitation, he picked up two bars from each of them and carefully made his way back to the knoll to join Otto.

It was full dark and the sheriff, with his two deputies were returning to search the mine for the Bauers. Walking up the old trail, filled with rocks and bushes without a light was a challenge. With a minimum of noise, they approached the pile of debris, the sheriff carried a powerful flashlight which he turned on and pointed toward the mine entrance. As he had before, the sheriff called for the inhabitants to come out, without any results.

Holding the light as far from his body as possible, the sheriff advanced on the mouth of the mine, flanked by his deputies.

"Anybody here," he hollered as he flashed the light around the cave.

"Looks like they ain't back yet, Sheriff," observed one of the deputies.

"You want to wait for them," ask the other.

The sheriff thought a minute before replying.

"Naw, I've wasted enough time here. Let's go home."

Tired but elated, the Bauers arrived at their jeep and drove on to their camp. Their elation was somewhat dampened with the discovery the next morning of their visitor's footprints.

"We gotta get out of here before that damned sheriff catches us here," Heinz complained. "We got some money. We're gonna check into an old motel and celebrate!"

"Can I get drunk, Heinz?" Otto quivered with anticipation.

"You can get drunk, Brother, as long as you don't get us throwed out of the motel," Heinz grinned. "We will pick up my Ford SUV and ditch the jeep."

In a short time the jeep was loaded and they were on their way to Tehachapi. Except for an additional coat of dust the SUV was much the same as they had left it. They wasted no time transferring their belongings from the jeep. Heinz made an effort to wipe his fingerprints off the jeep before abandoning it.

An old motel down town welcomed them, especially when Heinz paid two weeks in advance. They unloaded their gear and left it in the motel before heading to Bakersfield to pawn the other four gold bars.

Jethro paid out the twenty eight thousand dollars with little comment. The jubilant brothers did not notice that he followed them far enough to copy down the make of their vehicle and the license number. Back in his shop, Jethro went to his computer and looked up a telephone number for the Los Angeles County Police Department. He then closed and locked his shop and walked a couple blocks to a public telephone booth.

"I have information regarding the ransom gold that was paid to the extortionists," he told the woman who answered the phone.

"I need your name and phone number," the woman replied.

"Lady, I am not going to give you that. I want to talk to the man in charge of the case if you want my information."

"Just a minute, I'll see if Captain Walker can come to the phone."

There were a couple of clicks and a male voice came on the line.

"This is Captain Walker. What can I do for you?"

"Captain, I have the name of a man who is selling US Treasury gold bars, and I know the vehicle that he drives. I do expect to be paid for that information," Jethro explained.

"There is a reward of five hundred thousand dollars for information leading to the arrest and conviction of the one responsible for the poison threat of our water," Captain Walker responded carefully.

"I care nothing about the arrest and or conviction. That is someone else's problem," Jethro replied. "I have the man's name. Do you want it or not?"

"I'm sorry, I can't offer you the reward for just his identity," the captain answered.

"I will accept one hundred thousand dollars for his identity, no strings attached."

"I'm sorry," Captain Walker repeated. "I need to check with a higher authority for that. Do you have a phone number that I can reach you?"

"No, I don't! When can I call you again?"

"The day after tomorrow, about this time," Captain Walker replied. "I should have an answer for you."

There was a click as Jethro hung up.

"Did you get a tracer on him?" Captain was still holding the receiver.

"Yes, Sir. We should have a location in a second. Here it is. It's a phone booth on the corner of Seventh Street and Robin Avenue in Bakersfield," a woman's voice responded.

"Thank you, Rachel. Would you get on the internet and look for an assay office or a pawnshop, or any place that might buy gold? A place near that location."

Thirty minutes later, Rachel called the captain.

"Sir, the only thing within five blocks is a pawn shop. It's on seven sixty three Sparrow Avenue, two blocks from the phone booth. It's called just 'Pawn Shop.'"

"Thanks, Rachel. That was fast work. Could you get the Bakersfield Police Department on the phone? I'm looking for Chief Justin."

"Chief Justin, thank you for taking my call. This is Captain Walker with the Los Angeles County Police."

"How are you, Walker? Have you found the ones who perpetrated the poison lake debacle?"

"No, Chief, we haven't found the culprit, yet. I did just talk to a gentleman, who says he knows of someone selling US Treasury gold bars."

"Did you now? That is a step forward. Don't know who else that would have access to Treasury gold," Chief Justin replied. "How can I help?"

"Chief, the call came from a phone booth in Bakersfield, located on the corner of Seventh and Robin. There is also a pawnshop nearby. I thought they might be connected."

"That would be Jethro Eddington's place. I know he is buying stolen goods, but I haven't been able to pin anything on him. Any assistance in that area would be appreciated," the Chief answered.

"That would fit. Maybe you could do a 'round the clock' surveillance on the shop. It's a long shot, but the only thing available, at this point," Captain Walker suggested. "I have a man in your area who is also a US Deputy Marshall. He might be able to assist."

"That would help a lot. I'm always short on manpower like everyone else in this business. I'll photograph every face that comes out of the pawnshop. Maybe something will turn up. Have your man contact me."

"His name is Adam Waterman. He is sharp and a cool head in a physical confrontation. I surely do appreciate your cooperation on this, Chief."

"My pleasure, Captain." Chief Justin hung up.

GOLD DISCOVERED

Adam's phone chimed as he was approaching the Townsend mine. He checked the caller and replaced the phone. It was Captain Walker.

"Not important," he told Emily and returned his attention to the road.

"I love you," she responded, "but this engagement business is rather sudden. Give me a day or two to sort things out before we tell Dad."

"I don't know how it will come down, either. I just know that I love you very much, and will miss you every hour that we are apart," Adam replied. "But you take what time you need."

After Adam had dropped Emily off at the trailer, he dialed Captain Walker's number.

"What did you find out in Nevada," was Captain Walker's opening remark.

"Not much, Captain. The mine was abandoned, had not changed hands since the original filing some eighty years ago. The guy obviously has something to hide, so I left my name and phone number with the Refinery. They promised to call me when he brought in more gold quartz and give me a description. I think we should alert the FBI."

"The trip wasn't a total waste though," Adam continued. "Emily and I had a great time in Reno and she promised to marry me!"

"Whoa! That's great news. Congratulations! It's about time you settled down. Does she know that you're a cop?"

"Well, not exactly," Adam hedged. "I have told everyone that I work for the US Treasury."

"Not every girl would relish being married to a cop," the captain reproved. "Well, that's your problem. I have some news from this end."

Captain Walker proceeded to relate the details on the anonymous phone call and his conversation with the Bakersfield Chief of Police.

"I don't expect the commissioners to release one hundred thousand dollars without some assurance that the name is legitimate. If the caller was the pawnbroker and he is buying gold bars, he won't be interested in killing the goose that lays the golden eggs. He's not going to give me a name for nothing!"

"I'll drive over to Bakersfield first thing in the morning and see Chief Justin." Adam thoughtfully replaced his cell phone and drove on back to his motel room.

Rachel pushed the intercom button to Captain Walker's office.

"That man is on the line again, Captain."

"Thank you, Rachel. Good morning. This is Captain Walker, how can I help you?"

"Do we have a deal? You will pay me one hundred thousand for my info?"

"We will pay for your information. The way it works is, you give me the name of the suspect, we check it out that it is legitimate info, not just a neighbor that you have a grudge against or something similar, then we will release the money," Captain Walker answered.

"How do I know you will pay, not just take my info and tell me to stick it up my nose?"

"You can trust us. If you have something, we will pay."

"Well, I don't trust the cops and I'll keep my information," the voice declared and hung up!

Regretfully, Captain Walker replaced his receiver. "Maybe they will discover something from the surveillance."

Adam checked in with Chief Justin and was immediately introduced to Detectives Mickey Childers and Ross Wellington.

"I hope you don't mind working under Detective Childers. You all are pretty high rank to use for mere surveillance, but this isn't an ordinary situation. I expect you men to notice any and all unusual happenings. I want to nail this guy and find out who is selling Treasury gold to him." Chief Justin strode back and forth, chewing on a large unlit cigar, as he instructed the three officers before him.

"You men will report directly to me. Ross, I want a picture of every face that leaves that shop.

Detective Childers knocked on the door of the house across the street from the Pawn Shop.

"Good morning, Mister James. I am with the Bakersfield Police Department." He showed his badge. "The Department has need of your house for a couple of weeks. We will pay you one thousand dollars per week. Do you have a friend or relative whom you would like to visit?"

"Why yes. Chief Justin called me. We are all packed and Nettie and I are going to Anaheim to see our daughter," the elderly man who had answered the door, replied. "We have been waiting for you. Nettie made you a fresh pot of coffee, help yourself to the kitchen. There is fresh linen in the upstairs hall closet. Come on, Nettie, let's go," he call back to his wife.

Adam picked up two suitcases that were standing near the door, followed the couple out to their car, and watched them drive away.

Detective Ross pushed through the back door with an armload of camera equipment and proceeded upstairs to a front bedroom, which looked down on the Pawn Shop. Set on zoom lens, the camera would enlarge the patron's faces to an easily identifiable size.

"You got the first shift, Ross. How do you like your coffee," Childers called up the stairs.

"Half teaspoon of sugar, no cream," Ross responded. "Thanks."

It was mid-morning on the fourth day that the monotony was broken. Adam thought he saw a familiar figure walk into the shop. It was several minutes before the figure reappeared and was positively identified. Heinz Bauer!

"Childers, I have a hot one. There is an APB on this guy in connection with assault, murder, attempted robbery and kidnapping. Can we get a tail on him? His name is Heinz Bauer."

Without answering, Detective Childers pressed a button on his cell phone. "Chief, we have a known perp. Heinz Bauer. There's an APB on him. Waterman wants a tail, maybe we should hit the shop. He could be the source of the gold bars."

"Give me fifteen minutes to get a car at the back door of the shop and then hit the front door. I'll have a warrant there in a few minutes," the chief replied. "Give me a description of the vehicle."

Childers held the phone out to Adam. "Describe the vehicle."

Adam passed on the description of Bauer's SUV and gave the phone back to Childers. With Detective Childers in the lead, the three policemen burst into the pawnshop.

"Just leave the merchandise there on the table, Jethro."

"What is this? Where is your search warrant, Detective," Jethro inquired and casually covered a small stack of jewelry with a newspaper.

A scared looking teenager stood across the counter from him.

Ignoring the question, Detective Childers read him his "rights". At that moment a uniformed policeman entered and handed a sheet of paper to the detective.

"Here is my warrant, Jethro. Spread out and see what you can find, men," he said to the others. "Put cuffs on that young man, Officer. He looks like he is ready to run out the door."

"I want everyone to empty their pockets when they leave, Detective," Jethro sneered.

"You have nothing in here that any of my men want," Detective Childers flushed with anger.

"Large locked safe in here, Rich," Detective Ross called from a back room. "Shall I blow it open?"

"What about it, Jethro? You want to open your safe for us or should we do it the hard way?" Rich Childers smiled faintly.

"I'll open it, Copper. I got nothing to hide," Jethro replied shortly, and walked back to his safe.

"Nothing unusual, Rich," Ross reported. "Stack of money, some fancy jewelry and a loaded thirty-eight pistol."

"I got a permit to keep a pistol. Are you satisfied?" Jethro started to close the safe.

"Wait a minute," Adam interrupted, and blocked the closing of the safe door. "I know of a crook down in Long Beach. He had a false back in his safe. Let me check."

Adam saw a flicker in Jethro's eyes and knew he had guessed right.

"That one had a control button just above the door opening." Adam felt along the top of the opening.

His finger touched a small button and the back of the safe slid smoothly into the sidewall, revealing a second row of shelves. Numerous bags of jewelry covered the shelves plus a small stack of US Treasury gold bars!

"I've had those for years," Jethro began weakly, a defeated look covered his face.

Detective Childers clapped Adam on the back and pulled out his cell phone to call his boss.

"Chief, you got to see this! Bring out an inventory crew and an armored car," He announced gleefully and hung up before the chief could ask any questions.

Detective Ross wrung Adam's hand. "Nothing like having a big city cop around when you need him," he chortled.

"Put the cuffs on him," Detective Ross said to the uniformed officer, indicating Jethro.

Rich Childers returned to the front office, where the teenager waited nervously.

"You have the right to remain silent. Anything you say can be used against you in a court of law. You may call your lawyer, or if you do not have one and cannot afford one, a lawyer will be assigned to you by the court. Did you understand all I told you?"

"Ye-yes, Sir," the boy answered.

Rich removed the newspaper from the small stack of jewelry. Revealed was a gold brooch with a large ruby center, surrounded by diamond chips. Matching earrings lay next to it. Rich stirred the pile, uncovering several expensive rings. He looked up at the teenager.

"Now, you can demand a lawyer and fight us to avoid a conviction and I will throw the book at you. On the other hand, you can tell me where you stole these from, and I will try to get you off with only probation. Your choice."

"It-it was a b-big h-house on Wh-whippoorwill Avenue."

"House number?"

"Fo-forty-nine t-twenty two."

Detective Childers wrote the information down on his notebook and dialed a number on his phone. "Lila, will you run down the resident of four nine two two Whippoorwill Avenue? Have them come in tomorrow to identify some stolen jewelry. Thanks, Lila."

He turned back to the boy. "What's your name, Kid?"

"D-Dennis R-Rollison."

"Dennis, they can cure stammering. You look me up when the court releases you and I will help you. It's about time you found The Lord and a new way to make a living."

The boy's nervousness disappeared like a flash, replaced by an aura of hope.

"T- Thank you, Sir. T-that would be real c-cool."

"Those gems you brought in looks like around twenty thousand dollars, Dennis. How much was Jethro going to pay you," Rich asked curiously.

The boy's face turned red with embarrassment and anger.

"Two hundred and fifty dollars, Sir."

The wail of sirens announced the arrival of Chief Justin. He burst through the front door, his curiosity at its peak.

"Come on back, Chief, and look at this," Detective Ross called to him.

A smile of satisfaction passed over his face as the chief observed the handcuffs on Jethro, but his jaw dropped when his eyes fell on the gold bars.

"We would never have found them had it not been for our friendly big city cop, Chief. Look at this." Detective Ross pressed the button and the false back slid out to hide the gold bars and pushed it again to demonstrate the false back of the safe.

"You knew about these safes, Waterman?" The chief turned to Adam.

Adam spread his hands. "I saw one once before."

Chief Justin lifted one of the bars from the safe. "Where did you get these, Jethro?"

"Chief, I won those on a lottery, thirty, forty years ago," Jethro said earnestly.

Ross grinned and pointed at the bags of gems. "You win these in the same lottery, Jethro?"

Jethro remained silent.

"Okay, men. Pictures and inventory everything in the safe and pack them up for evidence," the chief exclaimed as his cell phone chirped.

"Chief, I followed this SUV to a small motel in Tehachapi."

"Great! I'll contact the County Sheriff and send a couple squad cars. We will pick him up."

"We might be in luck, Chief. He stopped at a liquor store for a bag full on the way to the motel."

"Keep an eye on them. I am sending Detective Waterman and Officer Keller to pick him up.

94

KIDNAPPED

Emily Townsend tripped gaily into the trailer house, came up behind her mother and gave her a big hug.

"You are mighty frisky for just coming back from a long drive, daughter," Marge said with a smile.

"Oh, Mom, I have such wonderful news," Emily bubbled.

"I could probably guess, but you tell me," her mother chuckled this time.

"Adam asked me to marry him," Emily announced.

"I presume you said 'yes'. That would explain your giddy behavior," Marge responded.

"Oh, yes, Mother. He is so much a man! I never met anyone like him. I just love him to pieces." Emily continued to bubble over.

"I hope your father is half as enthusiastic as you are." A cloud passed over Marge's face.

"Why, Mom. What could Dad possible disapprove of Adam about?"

"I don't know, Emily. Your father never liked anyone remotely connected with the government." The cloud remained on Marge's face.

Gilbert Townsend returned from Tucson that evening, but Emily could not bring herself to tell her father about her engagement to Adam. Somehow she felt the antagonism that existed between Adam and Gilbert. A couple days later, Gilbert took a pail of raw gold to Idaho, gold that was supposedly gleaned from the river.

"Here, daughter. Take this coffee and brownies to the men. Don't forget Martinez is up on the hill." Marge handed Emily a covered plate and a coffee pot.

"Sure, Mom."

Somehow, Emily's spirits lifted a bit when her dad was away. She first delivered the snack to Martinez and received profuse thanks for her efforts. Then she went through the big tent to the mine entrance. The noise was deafening!

Rusty, who was running the jackhammer, saw her first and shut down the machine.

"You and the coffee are a sight for sore eyes." He smiled as he relieved her of the coffee pot.

Wilson put down his maul and joined them. He had been feeding the Stryker.

Emily wandered around, looking at the quartz being extracted from the walls. She noticed the electric extension cord leading to the side room. It had become partially uncovered. She started toward the blocked off area.

Wilson moved over, placing himself between her and the forbidden area.

"Your father left instructions that no one goes in there. It isn't safe." His lips were smiling, but his eyes were hard.

"But the extension cord," she began, pointing to it.

"Left over from the last owner," Wilson interrupted and continued to block her way.

"I see." Emily turned back to Rusty, who was looking slightly flustered, and took the coffee pot from him. "Can I give you a refill, before I leave?"

On the way back to the trailer house, Emily reenacted the previous scene.

"That extension cord was new. Wilson was ready to use force to keep me from looking into that branch cave. Are they hiding something from Dad? I think I will come back tonight and see what Wilson didn't want me to find."

Dinner was a tense event that night. Emily felt Wilson's eyes on her but refused, to look at him. Marge was aware of the tension, but was at loss to know the reason. Everyone ate quickly and got up from the table without the usual chitchat.

Emily waited on her bed in the trailer house fully dressed. It seemed forever before the lights in the men's tent went out. She waited another half hour before venturing out. She carried a small LED light and a larger four-cell flashlight. She used the LED to find her way through the big tent to the mouth of the mine.

Emily turned on the large flashlight to illuminate the main cave. Everything was as she remembered it with the jackhammer lying next to the wall. The maul was leaning against the same wall and the Stryker sitting quiet in the middle of the room.

She turned her attention to the forbidden area, her heart beating fast as she advanced. She gave a gasp as her flashlight revealed the secret. Flicks of gold on the grinder wheel reflected the light beam and caused her confusion until she discovered the two pails of gold bars. She held one up to her light and read "US Treas" stamped on its face.

National newspaper headlines sped across her memory bank. "Southern California Water Supply Held Ransom for Four Thousand Pounds of Gold".

The operation was readily apparent to Emily's quick mind.

"Oh please, God, make it not so! My father was involved it that! My father is a crook!

A muted sob was wrung from her.

Suddenly she heard a sound behind her! She snapped off the light. The sound of gravel crunching under feet caused her to turn slowly and face the entrance. All was pitch black.

A blinding light flooded over her from a flashlight a bare five feet away. She heard a low laugh and opened her mouth to scream. A heavy pistol appeared in the light, pointed at her stomach.

"Scream and you're dead," a low menacing voice whispered, as she choked it back. "It must be Wilson. I'll wait until we are outside. They won't hear me in here."

There was a small sound as the intruder stepped to her side and reached into the pail for some gold bars.

"Outside," the voice whispered. "Make a sound and I'll kill you."

As the light beams left her face, Emily commenced to recover some vision, she moved carefully toward the entrance of the cave. By the time they attained the back of the tent, she could see the outline of her kidnapper. It looked too large for Wilson!

"Heinz Bauer"!

A scream rose unannounced from her throat, the first syllable escaped, before the heavy pistol crashed down on her head.

Heinz picked up the helpless girl and hid behind a bush as lights came on in the smaller tent. The light went out immediately and two figures slipped out of the tent carrying rifles. One faded into the shadows and the other moved around the glen with his gun held ready, guided by the starlight.

Heinz remained frozen with one hand over the girl's mouth to stifle any sound. He stayed hidden until the two-armed men returned to their tent and waited thirty more minutes.

Now he slung the unconscious girl over his shoulder and walked down the trail to his vehicle. Heinz shoved her in the back seat and used his bandanna to tie her hands behind her back. Then he drove back to the motel.

Leaving the girl in the SUV, Heinz unlocked the door of the motel and turned on the light. A loud snore from the couch guided his attention to Otto, who was asleep there. A whiskey bottle was clutched in his hand. Heinz reached down and took the bottle, noticing it still contained a couple of inches of liquor, he gulped it down.

He now returned to the vehicle and brought in Emily. He dumped her on one of the beds. Heinz then felt her wrist for heartbeat and gave a satisfied grunt when he found a pulse. Her hands had turned blue, so he removed the bandanna from her wrist. Looking around, he spotted the drapery cord, whipped out a knife and cut off a length off it. He then used the cord to retie Emily's wrists, using the other end to tie to a bed slat.

Casting a disgusted look at his brother on the couch, Heinz kicked off his shoes and fell, fully clothed on the remaining bed and went to sleep

The sun pouring through the front window woke Heinz.

"I need to sell these gold bars and get this girl out of here," he muttered to himself. "Damn fool, Otto. He's got to drink until he passes out."

He shook his brother roughly. "Wake up, Otto!"

Otto groaned and opened one eye.

"Otto. I got to go to Bakersfield. You have to watch the girl 'til I get back."

"Watch girl," Otto muttered and commenced to snore.

"Damn drunk?" Heinz slammed out the door.

Heinz did not spend much time chatting with Jethro. He passed over the four bars of gold and carefully counted and examined the cash that Jethro handed him. He returned to his vehicle, unaware of the eyes that followed. The unmarked police car that tailed him back to Bakersfield also escaped his notice.

Heinz stopped at the liquor store when he arrived in Tehachapi. He purchased two bottles of bourbon, some soft drinks and several bags of chips.

"A good stiff drink will wake that girl up and we can have a party!"

He drove on to the motel, grinning with anticipation.

Otto was showing signs of waking up as Heinz opened the door. He removed the cash from the old coat adding to his stash in his suitcase.

"We got over a hundred thousand dollars, brother." He told his sleeping brother exultingly. "A couple more weeks like this and we can retire for life!"

Heinz poured a generous amount of liquor in a plastic glass and added some cola.

"Need to sweeten it a bit for the lady," he remarked to no one in particularly.

He moved over to the bed and started to raise her up to offer her a drink. Her eyes were open and staring.

"Come on, Darlin. This will make you feel good."

Emily breathed in short pants, but showed no other sign of life

Heinz let the helpless girl slump back on the bed, his face flushed with anger.

"I suppose you're going to die on me," he muttered and put the glass to his own lips and drank it down with one gulp.

The pistol that Heinz habitually carried, tucked into his belt, was irritating his stomach. He reached down to adjust it when the door to the motel burst open.

Two uniformed officers, led by Detective Adam Waterman, leaped into the room with guns drawn.

"Don't anybody move," Adam sang out.

With his hand already on his pistol, faster than the eye could follow, Heinz drew his pistol and held it against Emily's side.

"You b_____ds, drop your guns or I'll kill the girl," he gritted out.

In one smooth motion, Adam swept his gun to eye level and fired. Heinz's right eye disappeared. He fell backward into the kitchenette and lay still.

"Cuff the one on the couch," Adam instructed Officer Keller. "I'll check on the girl."

"Oh my G-d, it's Emily! How did she get here?" Adam quickly checked her pulse. "She's still alive! Call the paramedics. Quickly!"

IN THE HOSPITAL

Gilbert had disposed of the gold nuggets at the Gold Processing Plant the evening before. He was just awakening from spending the night in a motel on the edge of Salmon City. His cell phone chimed.

"Gilbert, I don't know what to do! Emily has disappeared! I'm so frightened for her." Marge commenced to sob.

"Calm down, Marge. Tell me what happened." Gilbert felt panic rising in himself.

"That's just it, Gil. Nothing happened. She was just gone this morning. Her bed hasn't been slept in and her phone and purse are sitting on the nightstand. She wouldn't have left without them. She must have been kidnapped! Oh, my poor little girl!" Marge continued to cry.

"Now, Marge, I'm sure it's nothing serious, she is probably just taking a walk. I'll drive straight back. It is about sixteen hours, so it will be late tonight. Have the men circle the camp and look for footprints or car tracks. Call me if they learn anything."

Gilbert slowly put away his phone, then commenced to throw his things in his bag.

Gilbert climbed wearily out of his truck at ten thirty that evening. He was tired, frightened and angry. The rest of the camp was wide-awake, waiting for him.

"Marge, make me a sandwich of some kind and a cup of coffee," he requested of his wife.

"Now." Gilbert leaned against a tent pole, facing the others. "Do any of you know anything? If so, spit it out."

"Well, there is something, Boss." Wilson shuffled his feet nervously and continued to speak as Gilbert just stared at him. "Emily popped into where we were working with some snacks yesterday afternoon. She noticed the extension cord that goes back to the grinder. It keeps vibrating out from under the sand. She started to go back there, but I stopped her. I told her it was from the previous owner, but she didn't look convinced. She seemed awful quiet at dinner."

"We saw some boot tracks leading up the road a couple hundred yards," Rusty took up the story. "They were too big for any of ours. We think she got carried off!"

"I thought I heard something around midnight," Rusty continued, "Martinez and I got up to look around the camp but didn't see anybody."

Gilbert pounded the post with his fist in frustration.

"So, someone just walks into our camp and carries off my daughter! What kind of security system do we have here? Did he carry off our gold, too?"

"No, Sir. I checked, no one went down in the cave," Wilson declared.

Marge had arrived with a steaming cup of coffee and a tray of sandwiches. Gilbert calmed somewhat as he gulped them down.

"I couldn't get to the bank in time to get checks for you men. I was going to get them this morning. The nuggets came to one million seven and some change. You all will have to wait until the next load for your shares."

"Sir, I think I hear a cell phone, from the trailer." Martinez interrupted.

Marge ran for the trailer, arriving in time to answer Emily's phone.

"Who is this," she panted into the phone.

"Missus Townsend, this is Adam Waterman. I didn't have a number for you or your husband, so I tried Emily's phone. I have some bad news. I have just taken Emily to the Medical Center here in Tehachapi. She is unconscious from a head wound."

"Oh, thank God you have found her. She disappeared sometime last night, I have been worried sick. Where did you find her?"

"I will explain later, Missus Townsend," Adam's voice was thick with emotion. "She is in very bad shape. You need to get over here."

"Gil, Gil! They found Emily!" Marge ran from the trailer. "She is in the hospital. We must go see her!"

"Chief Justin is convinced that we have the extortionist," Adam later explained to Captain Walker, "but it doesn't fit somehow. Heinz Bauer just didn't seem clever enough to pull something like this off. Jethro finally admitted that he had bought fifteen Treasury gold bars from Heinz Bauer, the cash we found in Bauer's motel matches, but where is the rest of the gold? We found one hundred fifty ounces, almost ten pounds, but we are still missing almost two tons!"

"Back track him as much as you can," Captain Walker directed. "Maybe he stashed it in some mine. What does his brother have to say?"

"Otto doesn't have a clue. He is still recovering from a huge hangover. All he knows is his brother found the gold," Adam replied. "He can't be relied on as he appears to be missing some marbles upstairs."

"Keep plugging, Waterman. If any man can solve the puzzle, it's you. We still have that lead in Reno. Nesbitt, the FBI man, is staking the refinery out. I'm sorry about your fiancée. She needs lots of prayer. Keep in touch." Captain Walker hung up.

Adam met the Townsends when they arrived at the small Medical Center.

"Emily is in ICU. She was semi-conscious when I found her, in that she was awake, but unaware of her surroundings. Neither did she know me. We raided the motel apartment of Heinz Bauer and found her there. Bauer was killed. His brother was present, but had been drinking and did not even know that she was in the apartment. They are hoping he will remember some things, after he recovers from his drinking bout."

"I was present on the raid because I was the only one who could recognize Bauer," Adam explained.

"Will she be all right? Can we go in to see her," Missus Townsend inquired between sobs.

"The doctor is in with Emily now, Ma'am. He will brief us when he comes out," Adam replied.

"Do you know anything at all about how she got there, Adam?" Gilbert spoke for the first time.

"Not really, Mister Townsend. Her head is swollen, apparently from a very hard blow, probably a pistol. How or why she was in Bauer's apartment is a mystery," Adam responded. "No question she was there by force."

The door opened from the back and a man dressed in a green gown and cap walked in. He looked expectantly at them.

"Are you Mister and Missus Townsend?"

"Yes, yes!" Marge rushed toward him, choking back a sob. "Will Emily be all right?"

"I wish that I could answer that. I am Doctor MacFarlane. Your daughter is suffering under extreme trauma to the brain. There is very little that we can do except wait for nature to heal her. We have found it helpful to induce, with the use of drugs, a deep coma to reduce the brain stress. If the swelling grows any further we may have to enter surgically to reduce the swelling. Doctor Lenstein, a specialist in brain trauma is in Bakersfield and has agreed to drive here to examine her and do the procedure, if needed. We did not want to subject her to more travel."

"Doctor, how long before we know," Gilbert ask hesitantly.

"All I can say is that it is in God's hands. Probably at least a week, but it could be months. Sometimes they never recover. I wish I could be more positive. Just keep praying!"

"I need to go, unless you have more questions." The doctor commenced to edge away.

"No, thank you, Doctor MacFarlane. We appreciate your good work," Adam responded. "Could her mother go in to see her?"

"By all means. The girl will not, of course, respond in any way."

The three of them stood silently by Emily's bed. In spite of the many lines and tubes attached to her body, she seemed to be only asleep. Marge cried softly as she looked over her only daughter. Adam cleared his throat as he attempted to speak.

"Would you mind if I offered a prayer for her healing," he asked of the parents.

Gilbert and Marge looked surprised, but nodded their heads in assent.

"Our Father God. We know that Emily turned her life over to You and that she is Your child now. We ask You God for Your healing touch on her today, that she will be free from pain, and that You will restore her memory and her health in Your time. Thank You for listening to my plea, Lord. Amen!"

Adam opened his eyes to find both Gilbert and Marge with their head bowed. Marge had her hands folded.

"I need to go now," Adam stated and gave Marge a hug and Gilbert a handshake.

After Adam had gone, Marge leaned forward and took one of Emily's hands in both of hers.

"Was it worth it, Gil? If we lose Emily, all those millions in gold. Was it worth it," Marge struggled to maintain her composure.

Gilbert looked down at the toe of his boot as it followed the pattern on the linoleum, but said nothing, as Marge continued to cry. Finally, he broke the silence.

"I will try to arrange for you to stay here in an adjoining bed, Marge. I will sign the necessary papers to allow them to perform surgery, if necessary. I will leave the van for you and have one of the men come and pick me up." Gilbert touched his wife on the shoulder briefly, before striding away.

Marge did not react.

"Load the truck tonight," Gilbert instructed his men. "I want to leave for Reno at dawn."

"How is Emily doing, Boss?" Martinez was hesitant to bring the subject up.

"Not good," Gilbert replied shortly. "My wife will be staying at the hospital with her."

THE CHASE

FBI Agent Dick Nesbitt had been doing surveillance on the Reno Gold Refinery for two days. With two other agents, he had contacted the manager and explained the situation to him. The waiting room for their customers was on the second story, overlooking the giant refinery plant. The customers could watch the ore, which they brought in, being processed. First the ore was passed through a large grinder, reducing it into sand. From there it went into an enclosed vat, where the gold was chemically separated from the sand. Each station was meticulously cleaned after the ore passed through it, to ensure no gold was retained in the machine.

The miner, or gold seller, would back his vehicle into an unloading area, watch it unloaded, then go up to the waiting room. Depending on the amount he brought in, the process could take two to five hours. There were concession machines, free coffee and donuts to munch on, while they waited.

There was generally a short line of vehicles waiting to unload their ore and paper work to fill out, which added to their wait.

The refinery was open from nine o'clock in the morning until five o'clock in the afternoon. Agent Nesbitt and his men took three-hour shifts in the waiting room, hoping for a high sign from the receiver that the gold miner, supposedly from that old abandoned mine, had arrived.

It was mid-afternoon on the third day that Dick Nesbitt got a signal from the man at the receiver desk. A stocky man had just completed filling out the required form on where the gold ore had come from. Dick took out his cell phone and pretended to have a conversation on it. As the man came up the stairs, Dick snapped his picture with his phone camera. The man strolled over to the coffee urn and poured a cup of coffee.

"Need to get that coffee cup and get his fingerprints," Dick muttered to himself. "Also need Chuck and Willie to get over here. I can't arrest him, but I can follow him and find where the gold is really coming from!"

Gilbert Townsend arrived at the Reno Gold Refinery somewhat later than he had planned. A tire blowout had deterred him. Further, there were six trucks ahead of him for the unloading dock. Still, since his load of ore was already pulverized, his time at the refinery would be shortened.

"I should still be out of here by five. I hate to spend the night here. Maybe I'll go down the road to that little place I stayed at last time," he mused as he sipped the black coffee. "That guy at the counter looked at me oddly, when he examined my form. Did I slip up on one of the questions? That guy across the room looked at me three times while he was yakking on the phone. Aw, I must be getting paranoid!"

Gilbert settled down with a copy of "Field and Stream". He was on the lookout for a good spot to vacation after the ransom gold was all converted. He finished off his coffee and tossed the paper cup in a waste can. Now he needed to go to the bathroom. On his return he didn't notice that his coffee cup had disappeared. He did notice that although there were a dozen men in the waiting room, the man that had eyed him earlier was missing. Gilbert thought maybe the man's load was finished and he was getting his money from the receiver, but he wasn't at the desk either. Mystified, but not alarmed, Gilbert resumed his perusal of the "Field and Stream".

Having read three magazines, Gilbert checked his watch.

"Quarter to five. Am I going to have to come back tomorrow? Be a long day tomorrow if I do."

Just then, the man at the desk announced that his load was finished. Gilbert stood and descended the stairs. The man at the desk did not look at Gilbert, said nothing, but just handed him confirmation of the deposit into Gilbert's bank, one million, seven hundred thousand, three hundred forty-two dollars.

Gilbert thanked the man and strode out to his truck, a seed of suspicion stirred in his mind. He looked around the almost empty parking lot. There were eight dirty, dusty trucks parked there, probably miner's, several relatively clean pick-ups, probably employee's, and one late model sedan with tinted windows, which was parked farther away near the exit.

"Something is not right," Gilbert mused. "First that desk man looks at me like I had my shirt on inside out, and then this guy stares at me while he carries on a phone conversation. Come to think of it, his miner's clothes were almost brand new, then he disappears without picking up a check. Now, there is a car in the parking lot that reeks of unmarked cops! Five bucks says it will leave here right after I do!"

Before getting into the driver's seat, Gilbert moved his assault rifle from behind the seat to the front seat, wedging it in between the seats next to him. He chose a route to the parking lot exit that would take him past the front of the sedan. He wanted to see if the driver's seat was occupied. It was!

Fully convinced that an enemy occupied the sedan, either the police or a hijacker, Gilbert slid into a parking spot and pretended to be answering his cell phone. With his other hand he shook out a map of the local area.

"I need to lead them around until dusk and shake them after dark. Those Nevada license plates that I have on will fake them out. If they try to close in I'll use the rifle on them. I'll cut off north on route four forty-seven and take to the desert going through that dry lake bed. That sedan can't follow me in there. If I can't get to Lovelock via trails, I will backtrack to Fallon and take Highway ninety-five south. After they give up the chase, I will strip off the Nevada plates and check into a motel for the night. Maybe I can find a car wash and drive a clean truck. They won't recognize me if they do bump into me."

Gilbert drove sedately out of the refinery parking lot. The sedan waited a few minutes, then followed.

When Gilbert Townsend stepped out of the room and into the bathroom, Dick Nesbitt strolled by the waste paper basket. He dropped his pencil on the floor as he passed it and while bending over to retrieve the pencil, he snatched Gilbert's coffee cup from the wastebasket. Dick continued on over to the stairway and walked out of the building.

It was a short wait before a Chevy sedan drove into the parking lot and stopped in front of Dick. He climbed into the back seat, fished out a zip lock bag from under the front seat and stored the used coffee cup in it.

"I need to get his picture and these prints off to the main office," he mentioned to his two agents in the front seat, showing them the picture that he had snapped earlier.

"We should be able to find out, who we are dealing with. Here is the miner's picture. They waited nervously as miner after miner came out of the building and drove away, knowing that the fewer vehicles in the parking lot, the more apt they were of being noticed. It was drawing close to closing time when their quarry appeared. He walked over to a very dirty pick-up truck, milling around somewhat before getting in.

"Chuck, you have the glass, see if you can read the license plate," Dick directed.

"Its Nevada plates, Boss. Looks like NK372L. The plate is pretty dirty. That three could be an eight." Chuck responded.

The truck commenced to move and drove toward the entrance, passing nearby. Willie, who was behind the wheel of the sedan, reached for the switch to start the car, when the truck suddenly pulled into a parking spot.

"Looks like he is answering his phone," Chuck remarked.

Dick didn't respond as he was on his phone to his home office.

"Yes, Sir. We have the suspect under surveillance at this time in the parking lot. Could you run a make on the vehicle? Looks like a twenty eleven or twelve Chevy Silverado, light green, Nevada tag number NK372L, the three could be an eight. I'll send a picture as soon as I get off the phone and fingerprints later, when I get to my kit. Yes, Sir. Thank you. Good bye."

Willis reached forward and started the car.

"He's leaving now, Dick."

"Just don't lose him, Willis," Dick replied.

Never allowing more than a couple of cars between the sedan and the truck, The FBI had little trouble tailing the suspect. No effort was made by the truck to evade or shake them as they made their way through heavy evening traffic. The sun was down when the two vehicles finally headed north.

Dick's cell phone chirped.

"Dick, I have mostly bad news regarding the identity of the suspect. The Nevada license plate was stolen a month ago and came off a Toyota. The picture turned up no matches, so he apparently has no record. If we find him, it will have to be from the fingerprints."

The information from Washington was disappointing, but the stolen plates indicated that he was guilty of something and was not an innocent bystander.

"We are headed north on Highway four forty-seven, so much for Waterman's theory that he was from the Mojave region. The traffic is thinning, but it will be dark soon. He has shown no suspicion of being tailed, but with only a few of us on the road, he must catch on soon," Dick responded.

"If you lose him, the fingerprints are the only arrow left in your quiver, so get them to me ASAP.

"Yes, Sir. We will tail him as far as we can." Dick rang off.

Ahead of them the truck began to slow, braking almost to a stop. The FBI sedan and two other cars between them were forced to go around it. The truck suddenly veered off the highway, across the ditch and headed out across a dry riverbed.

Willis braked to a stop, watching as the truck also stopped. The darkness was such that the driver of the truck was barely visible, as he stepped out of his cab with a rifle in his hands. He proceeded to use the rifle butt to knock out all his taillights.

Then the truck started up again, to disappear into the darkness!

Dick pounded his fist on the seat.

"Damn, Damn! He faked us out. He knew all along that we were tailing him, planned it all out and played us for a sucker." Dick Nesbitt was furious. "Let's go back to the motel and check out those fingerprints."

THE COP

Gilbert Townsend drove carefully without any lights for a quarter of a mile before making a u-turn back the way he had come. He watched two of the three cars that were behind him continue on north. The third turned around and headed back toward Reno.

"That's the one that was chasing me. I'll just wait a bit and drive back to the highway. Driving out here without headlights is the pits. I'll end up breaking an axle on some ditch."

Gilbert had a restless night on a lumpy mattress of a seedy motel. His decision was that the men in the sedan were police of some sort. It was strengthened by the realization that Hijackers would be driving a vehicle capable of overtaking his truck in any terrain.

"Maybe it is time to draw back for a few months, let things cool off," he thought to himself. I've converted over twenty million so far."

His musings caused him to overlook the fact that he was doing fifteen miles per hour over the speed limit. The lights of a highway patrol car brought him back to reality!

He slowed his truck, but the mountain road prohibited his pulling off the road until he came upon a viewpoint. A low wooden fence kept the viewers from falling over a steep cliff. He pulled into the viewpoint. The patrol car stopped a few feet behind him and a uniformed policeman stepped out.

"You were going pretty fast for a mountain road. Let me see your driver's license and truck registration."

Upon accepting the license and registration slip, the officer continued. "All the glass is broken out of your tail lights. Have you been in an accident?"

"No, Officer. I made the mistake of staying at a fleabag motel last night. Someone didn't like the looks of my truck and used a club on my lamps," Gilbert replied. "I'll get it taken care of as soon as I get home."

"And where is home, Sir?"

"I live near Bakersfield, California."

At that point, the radio in the patrol car blared. "All cars, APB (All Points Bulletin). Be on the lookout for light green Chevy Silverado pickup. Has rear end damaged, probable smashed taillights. Expect armed resistance."

Seeing a startled look appear on the officer's face, Gilbert slid his hand to the pistol stuck in his belt. The previous pleasant demeanor vanished from the officer.

"Put your hands in sight and get out of the truck," he ordered, his hand reaching for his revolver.

Instead of obeying, Gilbert stuck his own gun out the window.

"No! You put your hands on your head and step back three paces." Gilbert then climbed carefully out of his truck.

"Turn your back," Gilbert instructed and removed the officer's revolver from its holster, when the officer obeyed.

"Now, take your left hand and remove your handcuffs from your belt and snap them on your right wrist."

A semi trailer rig roared by at that moment and instead of complying, the officer whirled and used the handcuffs to lash out at Gilbert, striking him in the chest. Gilbert responded by smashing the officer in the face with his pistol. The officer fell, his helmet coming off his head. As he struggled to rise, Gilbert crashed his pistol on the officer's forehead.

"You fool! Now what do I do? Got to get him out of sight before a car stops."

Quickly, Gilbert dragged the officer to the patrol car and sat him in the driver's seat, coming back for the helmet. He replaced the revolver in the officer's holster along with the handcuffs.

His eyes fell on his driver's license and registration slip lying on the ground and retrieved them.

He stopped a minute to collect his thoughts, his eyes fell on the wooden fence and the cliff beyond. He made up his mind!

First, he drove his truck forward a hundred feet. Next, returning to the patrol car, he reached past the unconscious police officer and started the car. Then he rolled down the driver's side window and shut the door. Now, reaching through the window, he turned the steering wheel to the right, toward the cliff and dropped the transmission into 'Drive'.

As the car began to move, Gilbert walked along side to steer it. With its powerful engine the car soon picked up speed until he had to run to keep up. As the car neared the wooden fence, Gilbert leaped aside and watched with regret, as the car crashed through the fence and disappeared over the bank.

A huge cloud of dust arose when a treetop broke its fall, as it crashed to a stop at the tree's base. A flame flickered, and then spread, culminating in a loud explosion. Gilbert ran to his truck and drove quickly away.

Several cars saw the column of smoke and pulled into the viewpoint to look. All traces of Gilbert's encounter were erased by the many tire tracks and footprints by the time the fire truck and the police cars arrived.

Out on the road, Gilbert cut over on Highway 6 to California 395 highway to Mojave. As soon as he was in California he stopped and replaced the stolen Nevada license plate with his own California tag. The Nevada tag he discarded.

In the middle of the night, tired and distraught, Gilbert drove into his camp and threw himself onto the bed, fully dressed. His restless sleep was interrupted at dawn by Martinez rustling around in the kitchen. Marge was still at the hospital with her daughter, Emily. Martinez had inherited the task of feeding the rest of the crew.

"Coffee will be ready in a few minutes, Boss," Martinez told the blurry eyed figure that came from the bedroom.

"Go tell Wilson to get up the hill on lookout and to expect trouble," Gilbert responded. "Tell him to take two rifles, plenty of ammo and to clean and oil them to make sure they are ready for action.

As a startled Martinez ran out the door, Gilbert poured a cup of coffee from the still perking urn and commenced to clean his own weapons. Looking out the window, he saw Wilson run up the hill with a belt of ammo over one shoulder and a rifle in each hand. Rusty and Martinez burst in the door each armed with one of the assault rifles.

"What's coming off, Boss?" Rusty appeared serious, even eager.

Gilbert took a sip of the hot liquid before answering. "The cops were waiting for me in the Reno Refinery. I had to run! Later, I was stopped by the Nevada Highway Patrol and had to kill him!"

A shocked silence greeted his statement.

"You killed a cop?" Rusty's remark was more of a statement than a question.

"First time I ever killed anyone." Gilbert's voice was a trifle thick.

"So, what do we do, now," Martinez questioned.

"It is time to cool it. You each have over a million dollars apiece. I just had a million seven hundred put in my account to split with you. We need to disappear for a few months, until the heat dies down. We will stay in touch with each other and come back and finish the job."

112

"But, Boss. We still have two-thirds of the ransom gold. What about that," Rusty wanted to know.

"It stays right here," Gilbert replied. "We will cave in the bank above the gold and dig it out, when we return."

"We really don't have any choice, we can't risk staying here and staying in business, they are too close. After breakfast, you two knock down the big tent and store it in the mine. Back the vans up and load the tumbler, the Stryker, the generator and all our tools in them. Sweep the off shoot clean as a hound's tooth, even the footprints," Gilbert directed. "I'll take some food to Wilson and clean up here."

With breakfast over, Rusty and Martinez departed to take down the big tent. Gilbert looked around the trailer.

"I'll come back later and carry away the food stuff and winterize the trailer. I need to get the machines and tools out of here and on the way to Colorado. I hope Emily is all right. I'll call Marge now." Need to spin a tale that she will believe.

"Oh, Gil, I'm so glad you are back." Marge was half crying. "Emily just lies there, barely breathing, and she is so white. The doctor looks grim and shakes his head. He says if she doesn't improve in a few days, he will send her to a large hospital in Bakersfield. I'm so frightened."

"I'm so sorry, Marge. I wish---." Gilbert let the sentence die. "You must be strong, darling. I have some more bad news. I had some trouble in Reno. I am closing the mine and sending the men and equipment back to Colorado."

"But, Gil! Why?'

"I will explain later, Marge. I need to go now. I'll see you in a couple hours. Good bye, Darling."

The men had the larger tent almost down when Gilbert joined them. Gilbert gathered up tent pegs and poles and stacked them near the mine opening, while Martinez and Rusty rolled up the canvass. Next, Gilbert backed one of the vans up to the mine entrance and the three of them started carrying out the machines. Soon both vans were loaded and driven a short distance down the trail.

The second tent was soon down and, along with the larger tent and stakes, was stored in the back of the mine.

"Martinez, go into the trailer and dig out a couple sticks of dynamite. They are in the small cabinet under the table," Gilbert directed. "Rusty, grab a flashlight from one of the vans."

When the flashlight arrived, Gilbert and Rusty descended into the small cave which contained the men's toilet and the stack of gold bars. They dug out an opening large enough to insert the stick of dynamite.

"Couldn't we take a couple of handfuls of bars with us, Boss," Martinez inquired, when he brought down the dynamite.

"No handfuls," Gilbert vetoed. "You can each hide one bar in your personnel effects. More than one would arouse suspicion. Take one for Wilson and have one last look!"

Gilbert inserted a stick of dynamite in the crevice he had made. After some consideration, he stuck the second stick in his hip pocket. He lit the fuse of the one in the crevice, they all scrambled out and ran back a couple hundred feet.

The muffled blast shook the ground, as a huge cloud of dirt and dust rose in the air and rocks pelted the onlookers so that they retreated further away from the blast. Only a couple feet of indention in the ground marked the spot where the ransom gold lay hid.

"I guess that's it," Gilbert said, after a long look around. "Wilson, you are in charge. Rent a spot in that mini storage place on the road to the cabin. Put both vans in under roof. You all have your own vehicle so transportation shouldn't be a problem. Try to act as if you are still poor while you are at the cabin, and don't attract attention. It may be a few weeks before I get there. It depends on how Emily does. It you leave, it is vital that we keep in touch. I don't expect to finish with the gold until next year. Good Luck!"

The three men filed by and each shook Gilbert's hand before climbing into the vans. Wilson was alone in the lead vehicle and Rusty drove the second with Martinez in the passenger side. Gilbert strode over to his pickup and opened the door.

The vans had driven only a few feet when a loud voice sounded from an electric bullhorn.

"Stop! This is the FBI! You are surrounded! Get out of the vehicles and stand with your hands on the hoods."

Wilson disregarded the order and gunned the engine, heading down the trail. His windshield shattered as a hail of rifle bullets struck it. Wilson slumped over, the van continued on, veered off to strike a large rock and stalled.

Both Rusty and Martinez rolled out of their van with assault rifles in their hands, Martinez running for a pile of rocks nearby. He stumbled as a man jumped up from cover and opened fire with his rifle. The man fell over backward when Rusty fired a burst from his rifle into him.

Somewhat screened from the rifles by his van, Rusty crawled to a small out cropping of rock. The cover proved inadequate as rifles from two sides finished him off. Surprised, with one foot in his truck, Gilbert grabbed his rifle and dashed for the mine entrance. Heavy bullets pinged around his feet as he bounded into the cave. All was quiet for a couple of minutes.

He saw a figure on the knoll where the Lookout had watched from.

FINGERPRINTS

Upon entering the motel room, Dick Nesbitt headed straight for the bathroom.

"Chuck, would you dig out my fingerprint kit," he asked before shutting the door.

"I drink too much coffee," he grumped, as he carefully removed the coffee cup from the zip lock bag.

Carefully, he dusted the cup, realizing all that depended on a good reading. He took several pictures of each portion of the cup, trying to leave nothing to chance. At last, Dick sat back in his chair and wiped the sweat from his forehead.

"That's as good as it is going to get," he remarked to no one in particular and pressed send on his IPhone. "Now we wait. Willis, would you run out and get us some sandwiches? I need to wait for them to email me the results."

Dick paced across the room, then turned to his suitcase. He removed a copy of the book entitled "Shell Shock", written by an old Marine.

"Might as well relax," he told Chuck. "It could take some time to find this guy.

Willis arrived with food and it was eaten in silence. All attempts to start a conversation were met with failure. Dick brought out his IPhone for the tenth time, willing it to ring, before going back to his book.

At midnight, Dick stood up and yawned. "We might as well try to get some sleep. Can't do anything at this time of night, even if we do get an ID (identification)."

The room lights had been out for five minutes when Dick's phone lit up. Dick answered on the first ring.

"Agent Nesbitt, your prints were good. I am sending a photograph, however, it was taken twenty-six years ago and may be of doubtful assistance. The name associated with the fingerprints is Gilbert Townsend. He was apprehended in a small Colorado town. His record was expunged because of his age, seventeen, but his prints remained on record. He gave an address of twenty seven sixteen West Raven Lane, Pueblo, Colorado. He either stayed out of trouble or escaped detection thereafter, as we have no further record. Perhaps the Social Security Office might help."

Dick snapped on the desk lamp.

"If you guys can sleep with this light on, go for it. I need to do some computer work."

Dick entered the White Pages and typed in "Gilbert Townsend", all states. He received forty-eight names.

"Let's see, he was seventeen and that was twenty-six years ago, that would make him forty-three. That matches the guy I saw yesterday. Now, there is a forty-one year old, a forty-four, and two forty-two year olds. The rest are too old or deceased. Gilbert Townsend, age forty-two, wife Marge and daughter Emily, in Canon City, Colorado. The other one lives in Maryland. Gilbert and Josephine, three kids, Gilbert Jr., Josey and Mary."

"I'll send this info to the boss and have him check those two locations with the picture that I took. I might as well send it to the Nevada, Idaho, California and Arizona State police departments. An APB might turn up someone who recognizes the name or picture."

"Boss, if you would quit jabbering to yourself, we could probably get to sleep," came a voice from one of the beds.

"All right, all right! I'll be finished in a few minutes," Dick growled.

Using his IPad, he took a picture of the data which he had collected and emailed them off. As an afterthought, he sent the same to Captain Walker of the Los Angeles County Police Department and Adam Waterman.

With a sigh of relief, he rolled back into bed and with a clear mind, immediately went to sleep.

With little for them to do, and having gotten to sleep in the wee hours of the morning, Dick Nesbitt and his agents slept in. They finished a late breakfast. Willis and Chuck were playing nickel slot machines and Dick was reading the local newspaper when his cell phone chirped.

It was one of the few times that Dick's supervisor sounded animated. "Bingo, Dick! Your Townsend in Canon City, Colorado, checked out. There were renters at that address. They identified the man in your picture as the Gilbert Townsend who rented them the house. They have no contact with him and deposit the monthly rent in a bank account. I am working on getting information from the bank, which may take some time.

"At any rate, we are a step closer! We will nail him eventually. Stay there or come back to Washington, your call. Has anything developed on those gold bars found in California?"

"I'll probably return to Washington," Dick responded. "I'll contact Adam Waterman to see if he has anything new. His finding those gold bars must be connected, maybe Townsend and Bauer are, or were, partners."

"Let me know."

Dick motioned for his men to join him. He passed on the information regarding Townsend.

"Unless I get something positive from Adam Waterman in Tehachapi, we will return to Washington. Chuck, get on your phone and check on the next flight to D.C., while I call Adam."

"Hey, Adam. How are you doing? Have you checked your email this morning?"

"Hi, Dick. No, I've been hanging out here at the Medical Center, hoping Emily would wake up. Have I missed something," Adam asked.

"Well, I think we have a name and photo of one of the characters involved in the Ransom Gold case," Dick replied. "We lost him last night when he drove off the road with his truck after dark and we couldn't follow him. I requested an APB of the surrounding state police, but don't expect any return for a day or two. Nothing I can do in Reno as he is not going to return here. I'm going back to D.C. unless you have something."

"I'm at a stand-still, Dick. I am sure the gold is near here, as Otto only knows that Heinz made three trips to get the gold bars. Heinz death pretty much put Otto over the edge, so I'm not sure we can rely on anything he says. And to be truthful, Emily being in a coma has me so screwed up, it is hard to concentrate on anything else."

"I'm real sorry about your fiancée, Adam. Let me know, if I can help, or if you can use me there."

Barely five minutes had lapsed when Dick's phone rang again.

"Dick, you can't be serious! I just read your email! Marge and Gilbert Townsend are Emily's parents! They can't be tied up in anything like that. Are you sure?" Adam was frantic.

"Did you look at the picture, Adam? Is that the guy you know?"

"Yes, that's Gilbert alright, but there must be some mistake!"

"Adam, there's no mistake. He drives a light green Silverado pick-up. He led us around for an hour waiting until dark, and then ditched us clean. I took his picture. I saw him up close. He cashed in one million, seven hundred dollars in gold dust that supposedly came from an abandoned mine! He previously brought in over four million. All in just a few weeks."

"I-I guess-. I can't believe Emily could be mixed up in something like that," Adam choked. "Gilbert bought a mine from an old prospector and immediately found a good vein, but nothing like that kind of production. It is beginning to make sense."

"Listen, Adam. Don't move on this until I get there. We will leave now and it will take us ten or twelve hours to drive there. Get the local sheriff involved. Maybe we can hit the mine tomorrow morning. And buck up, Adam, maybe your fiancée didn't know anything about it."

Adam slowly put his phone away. He couldn't face Marge just yet. He left the waiting room and made his way to his car.

The day dragged for Adam. While he was waiting for the sheriff to return his call, he googled up an aerial map of the mine area. Having acquired the coordinates to put into his GPS to pick up Emily, this was a simple task.

"Here is the knoll where he keeps his man on look out. We need to approach on foot and keep out of his sight." Adam reverted to his habit of talking to himself. "I'd like to get my Quad in close, in case somebody gets away on foot. We can pretty much block the trail. Now here is something. This picture was taken before the tents were erected. There is another mine entrance! The sleeping tent masked the entrance so I never noticed it when I picked up Emily. She didn't mention a second mine."

"This scale is too small. I'll go by the library and blow it up there."

The sheriff called while he was in the library and he put him on hold until he could get outside.

"Sheriff, thanks for getting back to me. We think we have at least part of the gang on the 'ransom gold' caper. Could I count on you to help raid the place tomorrow?"

"That's great news, Waterman. Where are we hitting and what time," the sheriff asked enthusiastically.

"I am expecting Dick Nesbitt with the FBI in tonight. He has two men with him," Adam replied. "The target is the old Jodie mine, presently owned by Gilbert Townsend. He has three men with him and assault rifles for weapons, so it will be no pushover."

"Oh. That was where that shootout occurred a while back, two dead bodies! There was a lovely lady, who seemed to be taken with you. Hope she isn't involved! Well, with my two deputies, that will be seven of us. We should be able to handle four city slickers," the sheriff answered confidently.

"How about we meet at my motel room tomorrow at eight thirty? Hopefully, Dick will be there by then."

"We will be there, Detective. Appreciate you letting us in on it."

With the more enlarged map, Adam was able to mark out a route for the men to approach the camp without detection. He also found a way to bring his Quad behind the hill containing the lookout man.

He made a copy for the sheriff and returned to his motel. All he could do was wait. He did not want to return to the Medical Center!

After a short meeting, the men loaded their weapons and started out. Adam drove his truck with the Quad, Chuck, the FBI agent rode with him. The sheriff took the rest in his SUV. They stopped a mile short of the camp to walk the rest of the journey. Adam and Chuck unloaded the Quad and followed the map to get as close as they dared.

They were still a quarter of a mile away, when they heard a loud explosion. A cloud of dust rose from their destination.

"Something is coming off," Nesbitt exclaimed. "Let's step it up."

They broke into a trot, still being careful to stay out of sight of the lookout.

Adam started cautiously up the hill as Chuck stood guard. He heard the vans' engines start up and then a fusillade of shots. Throwing caution to the wind, Adam ran the rest of the way up the hill. He could hear Chuck following.

Adam reached the crest in time to see Gilbert dodge into the mine. He spent a minute looking around, quickly assessing the situation. Three down and one to go.

He called down, "Gilbert, I'm on your lookout spot. You can't get away. Give up and throw out your weapons."

"Damn you! Is that you, Waterman, you dirty turncoat. Come down and get me!"

"You can't get away, Gilbert. You're surrounded. Your men are all down. It is only you left," Adam coaxed. "You will be driven out with tear gas. Even if you were to get out alive, I have my Quad. I will run you down."

Adam kept his rifle trained on the mine entrance as Chuck joined him.

"He has guts, he may run for it," Adam remarked.

At that moment, a lit stick of dynamite arced from the mine opening! The resulting explosion blew up a large cloud of dust. They glimpsed a figure running out of the mine, both opened fire, but the dust blotted out the runner.

Chuck started down the hill in pursuit, while Adam ran the other direction, headed for his Quad. He overtook Chuck just past the mine entrance.

"He ran down that trail," Chuck called, pointing to a faint path leading away from the mine."

Not wishing to run into an ambush, Adam drove slowly. He could see the footprints of the running man. He followed for almost a mile and could see that the runner was starting to tire.

Suddenly a bullet pinged off the frame of the Quad, and caused Adam to stop and leap off the other side. He saw a rifle barrel protruding between two rocks. His return shot chipped the rock an inch from the barrel.

"Gilbert, don't make me kill you. Think of Emily. You will have to spend some time in prison. At least you didn't cause any deaths."

"You're wrong, Adam." Gilbert spoke in a low monotone. "I killed a cop in Nevada- If they capture me, I'll get the gas chamber."

"Whaat!" Adam was shocked.

Gilbert was quiet for a while before speaking again.

"Adam, are you in love with my girl?"

"Yes, I am, Gilbert, and she has promised to marry me."

"Adam, you must believe me. Emily doesn't know anything about the ransom gold. She has been away at college and just dropped in unexpectedly. I swear, she is innocent of all my past. Promise me that you will keep her out of this and take care of her. And Marge, she just went along with me. She is not guilty of anything bad."

"I'll do the best I can, Gilbert." Here Adam's voice broke. "When Emily wakes up, I will continue to love and cherish her, regardless, and marry her."

"Thanks, Adam. That relieves my mind a lot. And tell Marge that I'm so sorry, and I love her!" A rifle shot punctuated his sentence!

Adam slowly stood up and walked to where Gilbert lay. It was over! Wearily, he picked up Gilbert's assault rifle and carried it back to his Quad. Using his cell phone, he called the sheriff. "We have another dead body, Sheriff. I'm headed back."

IN THE HOSPITAL

As Adam opened the door of the Medical Center, he faced the worst of tasks, the informing a person of their mate's sudden death. There is no soft way to tell them. Marge was in the waiting room when he arrived. Of that, he was grateful.

"Lord, be with Marge when I tell her. Give her strength to withstand the terrible news. But, Lord, may it be a turning point in her life that she may turn her back on crime, and even more important, that she turn towards You!"

Marge looked up as Adam crossed the room. She had been trying to read a newspaper to pass time. Her face was drawn and haggard from worry and lack of sleep.

"Adam, what's the matter? You look strange." Marge started to get out of her chair.

"Please, Marge, don't get up. I have some news." Adam took a chair next to her.

"It's Gil! Oh, please don't tell me it's Gil," her face began to twist. She held a hand out pleadingly.

Adam could only nod and draw her to him and hold her, as she broke into uncontrollable sobs. He did not attempt to speak.

"First Emily and now Gil. I can't take anymore," Marge sobbed.

After a while, her sobs subsided. "Where is he? Can I see him?"

"Not just yet, Marge. He is being taken to the morgue."

"Can you tell me what happened," Marge asked

"The FBI caught up with him, Marge. With the local sheriff, they raided his camp. Gilbert and his men chose to fight. They were all killed." Adam could not bring himself to reveal that he was also present.

Neither was he ready to tell her that Gilbert had taken his own life. Marge accepted his report without comment. It was as if that would be what she would have expected.

"Is there anything new with Emily?" Adam finally dared to ask.

"My daughter is in surgery," Marge's lips trembled. "They are doing a procedure to relieve the swelling on her brain. An expert from Bakersfield is here. It's been over two hours. They said it would take that long."

"I'll wait here with you if you don't mind, Marge."

"Please do, Adam. And thank you for coming to tell me about Gil." Marge was still fighting to regain her composure.

It was several more minutes of waiting. Adam leafed listlessly through a magazine.

The doctor was smiling when he did make his appearance.

"Your daughter is doing fine, Missus Townsend. I believe we made a good decision. Her vitals are already improving. She will be in Recovery for another hour or so. After that you can be with her again."

"Thank you, Doctor. Could you send someone to let me know when I can see her?"

"Of course, Missus Townsend." With a wave of his hand, the doctor retreated.

"Marge, I would like to offer a prayer for Emily's recovery," Adam said, after the doctor had departed. "Would you mind and would you like to join me?"

"Oh, yes, please, Adam. I don't have much connection with God these days. Please pray for Emily and me," Marge implored.

"Lord Jesus, we thank You for Your unfailing love for us. I know that Emily is Your child and that You want only the best for her. We ask, now, for a complete healing for her. That there is no loss of her mental faculties, and that she would have a renewed knowledge of You from this experience. We thank You in advance for Your healing touch. Now, Jesus, I give you Marge. For reasons that I don't know, she has never known You, but please fill her with a desire to join Your family. Give her peace in her time of extreme trial and give her back a strong and healthy daughter. Amen," Adam closed.

"God, I don't know much about praying," Marge prayed, "but if You will restore my daughter's health, I promise to follow You the rest of my life. Thank You, God."

"Thank you Adam for that. Somehow I feel reassured, as if Emily will be fine now. I am so glad she found you." Marge wiped her eyes and put on a weak smile. "I knew that they would catch up with Gil someday. Gil was so bright! He could have made good money at anything he chose without crossing the law, but he always dreamed of the big coup! He almost made it." Marge caught back a sob and wiped her eyes again.

"I knew what he was doing wasn't right, but Gil was my husband, and I loved him. I know I am going to have to go to jail for my part," Marge continued. "I've always known it would happen someday."

Adam squeezed her hand in sympathy. There was nothing he could say. His phone had chirped, telling him that he had a text message. He stood up.

"I'm so sorry, Marge. I must go. I will try to get back before visiting hours are over."

"Please do, Adam." Marge stood with him.

She gave him a hug and watched him leave.

Adam checked his message as he was leaving the Medical Center. It was from Dick Nesbitt, telling him that they needed him out at the sheriff's office. He hurried to his truck.

WHERE IS THE GOLD

"Look at this," Dick exclaimed excitedly.

They had searched the dead men and emptied their suitcases, separating each in a separate pile. On top of each pile was a gold bar and a checkbook.

"Each of the three men had a bank account off shore with over a million dollars on deposit. Townsend shows almost sixteen million off shore and two million in a Reno bank," Dick went on. That totals almost twenty-three million dollars. We couldn't find a sniff of gold anywhere in the mine. Where is the other three thousand pounds of ransom gold?"

Adam's mind went immediately to the Google map that showed a second mine. He opened his mouth to speak and closed it again.

"I'll bet it is covered up in that second mine. That was the explosion we heard. Marge must know where the gold is. I'll keep my mouth shut, and maybe the FBI will make a deal with her: No jail time in return for telling where the rest of the ransom gold is hidden!"

Dick looked at Adam keenly. "You were about to say something. You got an idea?"

"As a matter of fact, I do, Dick. We haven't had any time to trade information since you got in. I need to bring you up to date," Adam responded.

He proceeded to relate the happenings that led up to his engagement to Emily, the subsequent discovery of the gold bars with the pawnbroker and the raid on the Bauers.

"Emily," he finished, "is still in a coma, how she got to Bauer's motel room is still a mystery. Her mother, Townsend's wife, has been at the hospital ever since, waiting for Emily to awake."

"Wow, Adam! That puts you in a spot," Dick responded. "We need to pick up Missus Townsend right away. She must be an accomplice!"

"Well, let's think about this. I don't think she had much to do with acquiring the gold or converting it to cash, but, I'll bet she knows where they kept it. Couldn't we plea bargain with her? She tells us where the gold is, and we agree that she gets no time in prison. I can guarantee to bring her in whenever it is necessary," Adam added.

"Townsend could have moved that gold anywhere," the sheriff chipped in. "He was no dummy. That's a lot of gold. We have a couple of real good attorneys here in town if you need an agreement drawn up."

"I don't think I can allow Missus Townsend to just run around loose," Dick declared. She might decide to run. Regarding the plea bargain, I'll have to check with my boss."

The sheriff snorted. "Decide to run? This lady's husband is dead, her only child is in the hospital, laying in a coma, she has no wheels and the only money she has available to her is in her purse! And you're afraid she will run!"

"I don't know any of that." Dick Nesbitt's feelings were plainly hurt. "I need to put her under arrest."

"Well, I'm the sheriff here. This is my county and my jail. I'll decide who gets arrested here." The sheriff was taking this personal.

"Come on, Sheriff. You know I have the authority to make arrests here or anyplace in the country." There was anger in Dick's voice now.

"Not and put her in my jail. It is completely filled. Not a single cell empty!" The sheriff smirked, obviously lying.

"Come on, Guys. This is getting out of hand. Dick, we need to cooperate with each other. There is three thousand pounds of gold lying around here somewhere. That's close to sixty million dollars' worth! If word of this gets out the countryside will be full of treasure hunters. We don't want that." Adam's voice was soothing. "I have some authority as United States Deputy Marshall. I honestly don't know whether you out rank me or not, and I don't care. I will take full responsibility for her security."

"Why don't you just get on your phone and talk about a plea bargain," Adam continued. I will introduce Missus Townsend to an attorney and see if we can work this thing out."

"Adam is right," the sheriff intervened. "I apologize for getting in your face. I don't want to have to deal with a couple thousand strangers digging up the place. Let's get Missus Townsend to tell us where the gold is hid and get it moved back to Fort Knox, pronto."

Dick just nodded, removed his phone and started dialing.

Adam left Attorney Craig Newton in the waiting room of the Medical Center while he located Marge Townsend. He found her in Emily's room, as he expected.

"Oh Adam, I am so glad to see you," Marge whispered as Adam walked in. "The doctor thinks she is recovering. He says that all her vitals are better and she should be waking up, possibly in the next couple of days. I think your God is answering our prayer."

"Aw, that's great news, Marge." Adam walked softly over to Emily's bed and touched her on her white cheek.

"There is someone in the waiting room whom you need to meet," Adam said softly, returning to Marge's side.

Marge followed him from the room to the waiting area where the attorney was looking through some papers. The attorney stood as they entered the room.

"Marge, this is Attorney Craig Newton. I need to tell you, that besides working for the Treasury Department, I am a United States Deputy Marshall and a Detective with the Los Angeles County Police Department."

Marge looked at him in shock. "You are a policeman?"

"Yes, Marge, I am formally placing you under arrest." Adam went on to recite her 'Rights' to her. "You are not going to jail, but will remain in my custody until such time that the court instructs me otherwise. I have brought you Attorney Newton to represent you, if you so desire. He comes highly recommended."

"Missus Townsend, I am glad to meet you, but sorry it must be under these circumstances. I am prepared to represent you 'pro bono', which means without charge. Are you comfortable with that?"

"I-I guess so. I-I didn't expect--. I didn't realize Adam was a policeman," Marge stammered.

"I apologize, Marge. I didn't realize being in law enforcement was an issue with your family until a couple days ago," Adam responded. "I was sent out to find the ransom gold and catch the ones responsible. Gilbert was exposed while trading gold for cash in Reno then tracked back to his mine."

"I think, Missus Townsend, having Detective Waterman in law enforcement and on your side will be a definite advantage to you." Attorney Newton smiled at her. "We need to discuss some aspects of the charges against you. We could do so in private or with Detective Waterman present. What is your desire?"

"I can step out to Emily's room, Marge," Adam inserted.

'No, no, Adam. I would feel much more comfortable if you stayed."
Adam nodded and indicated a seat. They all sat down.

"Now, Missus Townsend, there has been no charges filed against you, but at the very least, they will charge you with an accomplice to Grand Theft or Extortion. Due the magnitude of the money involved, it will be a high profile case," the attorney began.

"I have been informed that a large amount of ransom money, or gold, has yet to be discovered," the attorney continued. "There is a chance, it is just a chance mind you, that there could be some reduction in your penalty, if convicted, if you were able to locate the missing gold for them. Would you be interested should they approach us with such a proposition?"

"Oh, yes, Sir. I--." Marge was interrupted by Attorney Newton.

"Ah, Missus Townsend, I need to remind you that anything you say in front of the detective could be used against you. For the maximum leverage for an agreement, you should seem reluctant to divulge the location of the gold. A simple yes or no would be an adequate answer to my question."

Marge understood. "Then I will answer, yes, Mister Newton."

"That concludes what I needed to discuss at this point, Missus Townsend, unless you have some questions for me." At Marge's shake of her head, he continued. "Here is my card. My office is only a few blocks away. It would please me if you will call me Craig."

"Of course, Craig. And my name is Marge." Marge offered her hand as they stood up.

"Adam, am I going to have to go to jail," Marge asked tearfully, as the attorney went out the door.

"I don't know, Marge," Adam said truthfully. "I am going to do all I can to prevent that. The FBI wants to locate the ransom gold ASAP. You can tell them. That may make the difference."

"But Adam, you know where it is, don't you?"

"No, Marge. I don't know where the gold is. I suspect that I could find it very quickly, but we won't discuss that with anyone," Adam replied. "Just try and relax and let Attorney Newton do his job. Take care of Emily, I will come back as soon as I am free."

Adam answered the phone on the second ring, as he strode to his truck.

"Adam, this is Dick. Does Missus Townsend have an attorney?"

"Yes, Dick. She does. Wait until I get to my truck, I'll get his info for you. Okay here it is, his name is Craig Newton, phone number, eight hundred-three six seven-nine nine six seven. What is new?"

"Our attorney will contact him and try to work something out. My boss is hot to get that gold back to Fort Knox before we have a gold rush on our hands," Dick responded. "I hope you can use your influence to help resolve this."

"I'll do the best I can, Dick. How about meeting for a late dinner, tonight about eight?"

"Adam It's a deal. At the café, next to our motel."

"What do you think, it will take for Missus Townsend to tell us where the ransom gold is hidden? How about no more than five years in prison?" Dick and Adam were waiting for their dinner to arrive. "Well, this is for the attorneys to hash out," Adam replied. "But my personal opinion is that she will not accept any prison time at all. Attorney Newton will soon discover that you really don't have any evidence to prove that Marge was even aware of the gold's existence, and if she does know the location and tells you, that is an admission that she is an accomplice."

"Oh, come on, Adam. She couldn't be married to him and not know that her husband picked the pocket of Southern California for eighty million dollars!"

"We don't know that, Dick. Stranger things have happened. And still, you have to prove that she knew, in order to show her as an accomplice," Adam maintained. "If I were her attorney, I think I would tell her to keep mum and request a dismissal due to lack of evidence."

"But, Adam, we've got to recover that gold!"

"Then I would convince your bosses to take hat in hand to Missus Townsend and ask her nicely, 'would you tell us where the gold is if we agree not to bother you anymore!" Adam smiled at his own humor.

Their food arrived at that moment and ended their discussion for now.

Next day, Dick phoned Adam. "I guess my bosses saw the light! I have been instructed to contact Attorney Newton and arrange whatever is necessary to locate the ransom gold. Also, I have my guys blocking the trail to the mine and everything is cleaned up. Missus Townsend can go back to her trailer if she desires."

Adam accompanied Marge, at her request, to the meeting with Attorney Newton and FBI agent, Dick Nesbitt. The attorney presented to Agent Nesbitt a contract agreeing to not press charges for any of her or her husband's action. It further limited governmental claims to bank accounts in her husband's name only and exempts any joint accounts.

"Any of the bank accounts that include your name as a signature are not to be claimed by the government," Craig Newton explained to Marge.

"So they won't take the money I have in savings in Canon City," Marge inquired.

"That's correct, Marge," Craig replied. "We have an agreement," he said to Agent Nesbitt.

Dick Nesbitt quickly signed the document on behalf of the FBI.

"If you know where the gold is, Marge, you may divulge that information," the attorney advised her.

"Well, I never actually saw any of the gold," Marge began. "I think it is in the second mine the one, they used as the men's rest room."

"Second mine?" Dick looked confused. There is only one mine there."

"Dick, do you remember the explosion we heard while we were getting in position. I think Gilbert dynamited the second mine entrance," Adam intervened.

"There were two mines," Marge reiterated.

"Google will show us where to dig. I printed out a map," Adam added.

Dick looked at Adam suspiciously. "I am getting an inkling that maybe we didn't need Missus Townsend after all.

"It's Biblical. 'Ye ask not, ye receive not." Adam grinned. "We need to enlist the sheriff to get us a back hoe tractor out there. Don't you think we should get some fire power to protect the gold?"

"I think, we could get a platoon of Marines from Camp Pendleton. I'll make a call," Dick responded.

Once it was in position. the backhoe made short work of finding the gold,

"Only dig where it is soft," Adam instructed the operator. "If you hit solid rock, you are out of the area. The dynamite should have broken the ground up."

Thirty-eight young men in camouflaged clothing surrounded the site with a light machine gun set up on the knoll. Their job was to prevent any of the gathering crowd of onlookers from coming onto the campsite. One, a First Lieutenant with a silver bar on his collar, stood with Dick and Adam observing the backhoe dig.

Only a few large shovels full of sand and rock had been brought out when the operator felt some resistance. He raised the shovel somewhat and carefully scooped some loose sand away, motioning for Adam to go into the hole and check.

Adam dug quickly around with his hands, and with yell of triumph, held up a gold bar!

The Lieutenant motioned over a truck and half a dozen men. The men formed a line and soon the gold bars were coming out of the hole and into the truck, while Dick, Adam and the sheriff stood by, grinning and congratulating themselves!

EMILY WAKES

A smiling nurse met Adam and Marge at the reception desk.

"Doctor MacFarlane thinks your daughter is coming out of the coma, and that she is sleeping. He expects her to waken anytime now. She will undoubtedly be disoriented and may not recognize you immediately. I will be back in her room in a few minutes. You may go on in."

Marge and Adam went quietly into the Intensive Care Ward and found Emily's room. As they had each morning, Adam laid his hand on Emily's forehead and prayed to God for her recovery. Adam pulled the only chair up next to the bed for Marge and seated himself on an adjoining bed.

Emily had many wires and tubes attached to her, but seemed to be breathing more natural. The machine, which monitored her heartbeat, showed a steady beat. Her hand twitched slightly and her lips moved, as if she were speaking, but her eyes remained closed.

The nurse who had met them, entered and joined a second nurse at a desk nearby. She checked Emily and the monitors first, then gave a smile of encouragement to Marge and Adam.

It had been a week since the ransom gold had been recovered. Captain Walker, overjoyed with their success had granted Adam time off "for as long as was needed" to stay in Tehachapi, until his fiancée recovered.

The government had seized all of Gilbert's and his men's off shore bank accounts and the one in Reno, Nevada. Marge had, however, through the agreement on revealing the location of the ransom gold, retained a substantial amount of money in her Canon City Bank.

The used car lot still had the BMW that Gilbert had traded in, so she was pleased to be able to buy it back. In an area where four-wheel drive vehicles were prevalent, the dealer was happy to get rid of it. Adam had taken her back to the mine camp to gather up her and Emily's personal belongings from the trailer house, as the government had also confiscated the mine itself. Marge had rented a small apartment, not far from the Medical Center.

While sitting with Emily, Adam studied a book on semi-precious stones, related to his hobby. It also helped to pass time.

It was mid-afternoon, Marge was napping in her chair, when Adam heard a noise from the bed. Quickly, he hopped up and stood over Emily. Her eyes were open and she was licking her lips!

"Nurse Philips, Emily is awake," he whispered loudly.

The nurse walked over with a glass of water. Expertly, she raised Emily's upper body with the electric motor and inserted a plastic straw in Emily's mouth. Emily sucked greedily on it.

"Not so fast, Dearie," the nurse crooned. "You are gonna be fine now."

"She will need to sleep awhile longer, before she really wakes up," the nurse confided to Adam. "When she wakes again, she will be real thirsty, but don't give her more than half a glass. After about ten minutes, let her have some more."

Adam elected to let Marge sleep. When Emily woke up completely would be sufficient. He knew Marge was having trouble sleeping at night. Her world had turned upside down in a very short period of time.

Visiting hours were almost over, when Adam heard a low moan from Emily. He stepped over and offered her a half glass of water. She quickly emptied the glass. Her eyes asked for more.

"Wait a bit, Darling, then you can have some more," Adam told her.

Emily moaned again, reaching up to touch her forehead.

The nurse was there, holding a hypodermic needle.

"You poor dearie. You must have the mother of all headaches. This will stop the hurting and let you sleep again. It will feel better when you wake up."

"You both might as well go home," the nurse said, turning to Adam. "This shot will put her out for the night. She will be better tomorrow."

Adam shook Marge's arm gently.

"Marge, we need to leave now. Emily kind of woke up, at least she opened her eyes and moaned some. She must be hurting a lot. The nurse gave her a pain killer and thought she would be better tomorrow."

"Oh, dear! Did she know you? Did she say anything? I'm sorry, I fell asleep." Tears came to Marge's eyes.

Adam just shook his head. He was too choked up to speak.

It was morning, the late shift nurse was making a last round, visiting the patients in Intensive Care. Emily was awake when she stopped by, so the nurse cranked up the head of the bed and fluffed the pillow. Emily's eyes followed her, but she said nothing. Suddenly, she spoke, her voice barely above a whisper.

"Are you- my mother?"

"No, Dear. I am Nurse Lila," the nurse answered, giving her a drink of water.

"I heard- my mother- talking- to me, but I- couldn't see- her. I don't-know, what- she looks- like." The whisper persisted.

"Your mother will be here in a little while, Emily. You are feeling better, would you like some breakfast?"

"I don't- know." Emily seemed to drift back to sleep.

Adam and Marge arrived in time to chat with Nurse Lila before she got off duty. She repeated the short conversation to Marge.

"What did she mean, she doesn't know what I look like?" Marge was distressed.

"Well, some believe that even in a coma, people can hear and understand conversation. But you can't take what your daughter says seriously, when she is coming out of a coma," the nurse soothed. "Hopefully, she will improve a little each day."

"The fact that she spoke at all is a good thing, isn't it?" Marge wanted to be encouraged.

"Oh definitely! She will probably waken again in a few hours and talk to you," the nurse agreed.

It was well past mid-morning, when Emily stirred and opened her eyes. She focused on Marge immediately and kept her eyes on her even while drinking water.

"Are you my mother," she asked. Her voice was weak and raspy.

"Yes, Emily, I am your mother." Two tears rolled down Marge's cheeks as she stroked her daughter's face. "I'm glad." Emily closed her eyes for a moment. "Why are you crying, Mother?"

"You have been gone a long time, Emily dear. I am just happy to have you back."

"Oh." Emily closed her eyes, seemingly to sleep.

All was quiet except the hum of the air conditioner and the drone of a telephone conversation at the main desk for about twenty minutes. Marge stepped back to wipe her eyes. Emily spoke again.

"Mother, are you still there?"

"Yes, Dear. I'm here."

"Could you hold my hand, Mother? I'm so tired."

"I'll stay right here with you, Emily. You go to sleep now." Marge pulled her chair closer to the bed and picked up one of Emily's hands.

Adam had been sitting on an adjoining bed during this exchange and was aching to join in, but something held him back. He felt that she might become more confused if he dealt himself in.

Emily slept most of the day, waking every hour or so to reassure herself that Marge was beside her. The nurses kept repeating that sleep was the greatest healer, Adam found himself in prayer a goodly part of the time.

When visiting hours were over, Emily was awake and seemed to understand that Marge would have to leave her, but would return tomorrow.

The next day was a turning point. Emily seemed more alert, slept very little and started to become aware of her surroundings. Marge explained that she had been injured and was in the hospital. She also discovered Adam, although she didn't speak to him, her eyes followed him when he moved or walked.

It was the third day after Emily awoke that was a red-letter day for Adam! That something about him was bothering her was apparent when he entered the room.

"Adam," Emily questioned tentatively, then "Adam, oh, Adam, it's you," she cried, raising both hands toward him.

Adam rushed to her side, bending to kiss her, as she clasped her arms around him! Tears of happiness flowed down her face.

"Welcome back, Darling." Adam finally pulled free enough to speak.

Marge joined them laughing and crying. Suddenly, Emily's face clouded over and fear leaped into her eyes.

"Heinz Bauer!" It was barely a whisper. Her body began to shake!

"Emily! Emily, it's all right," Adam soothed, holding her tightly. "He's gone, Darling and will never bother you again."

Slowly Emily relaxed, then tensed up again as memories returned.

"He was in the mine, he--. The gold! There were gold bars! My Dad! My dad is a crook!" Emily began to sob uncontrollably.

Marge now began to cry also. "I'm so sorry, Emily. I'm so sorry."

Adam just held them both, until the sobbing subsided.

It took another day of recovery before Emily could talk about her ordeal without crying. Adam and Marge discussed how and when to break the news of the raid on the camp and her father's subsequent death. They decided the sooner the better.

Emily was free of most of the wires and tubes and was able to sit up in bed. She made room for Adam to sit on the side of the bed. He took her hand in his.

"Darling, we have more to tell you. You need to brace yourself," Adam began gently. "Your father was detected selling gold in Reno from a fictitious gold mine. They traced him back to here and attempted to capture him and the others. They chose to fight and were all killed."

"My father-, then he is dead?" Emily fought for control.

"Yes, Emily." Marge took over. "Your father wouldn't have been able to stand being locked up." She took Emily's other hand.

"Your father wasn't a bad man," Marge continued thickly. "He was just greedy for a lot of money. He was so brilliant, an honest job was too easy, too tame. He always talked about making one big score, he called it. I know it wasn't right, but I loved him."

Marge sobbed quietly.

LAXTV

"Three days ago a combined force of the Kern County Sheriff's Department, the FBI, and a United States Deputy Marshall raided a suspected hideout for the gang, who held Southern California Water Authority hostage for eighty million dollars in gold.

"Here is Carl Lund to tell you about it. Carl?"

"Thank you, Irwin. Seven law enforcement officers descended on the site of an old gold mine near Tehachapi, California, in an attempt to capture suspect Gilbert Townsend. Townsend is suspected of masterminding the extortion of eighty million from the Southern County Water districts. The ensuing shoot-out left a deputy sheriff dead, one FBI agent wounded and Townsend with three cohorts also dead."

"Three thousand pounds of gold bars were recovered on site plus bank accounts totaling over twenty three million dollars!"

"The FBI reported that most of the gold was recovered, including the bank accounts should almost equal the total ransom."

"Captain Bradley Walker of the Los Angeles County Police Department was quoted as saying, 'the responsibility for tracking down this monster can be mostly credited to the intelligence and tenacity of Detective Adam Waterman. He single handedly searched Los Angeles and Mojave County for gold mines until he found the right one. I believe he has every right to claim the five hundred thousand dollar reward!"

"I talked to Detective Waterman on the phone and he modestly credited the organization of the FBI and Agent Dick Nesbitt for his success."

"Back to you, Irwin."

"Irwin Clayman again. Detective Waterman has remained in Tehachapi at the bedside of his fiancée, who was badly injured, partly because of the investigation. Upon his return, Mayor Whipple of Los Angles is planning a gala dinner in Waterman's honor."

138

"The Police Commissioner has already recommended Detective Waterman to be promoted to Lieutenant. I, Irwin Clayman, intend to make it my personal crusade to see that this young man receives the reward money

EPILOGUE

Emily refused to get married until all the bruises on her face disappeared and some of the hair had grown over the bald spot on her head, where the doctor had shaved.

Eventually, they had a quiet wedding at the "Shepherd of the Hills Church". Adam and his bride spent their honeymoon on Santa Catalina Island before Adam went back to work with the Los Angeles County Police Department.

Marge returned to her home in Colorado. She fulfilled her promise to the Lord to serve Him, ultimately joining a prison ministry at the nearby Women's Correction Facility.

Lieutenant Adam Waterman shared the reward money with the widow of the deputy sheriff, who was killed in the raid and some with the injured FBI agent. The balance was used to buy a small modest ranch in the hills, north of Los Angeles.

Emily became too busy to pursue her college studies in chemistry, being surrounded with livestock and later joined by a lively young boy.

www.ingramcontent.com/pod-product-compliance
Lightning Source LLC
Chambersburg PA
CBHW071126250626
47159CB00006B/2147